Private eye Noah Braddock has finally found peace in his once tumultuous relationship with Detective Liz Santangelo and has called a tentative truce with his alcoholic mother, Carolina. So when lawyer Darcy Gill demands that he look into a hopeless death row case, he's more interested in catching some waves before San Diego's rare winter weather takes hold. Then Darcy plays her trump card: the man scheduled to die—convicted of killing two men in cold blood—is the father Noah never knew.

LIQUID SMOKE

LIQUID SMOKE
Jeff Shelby

TYRUS
BOOKS

Published by
TYRUS BOOKS
1213 N. Sherman Ave. #306
Madison, WI 53704
www.tyrusbooks.com

Library of Congress Cataloging-In-Publication Data has been applied for.

15 12 13 12 11 1 2 3 4 5 6 7 8 9 10

(hardcover) 978-1935562399
(paperback) 978-1935562542

For Hannah Elizabeth

The Last Day of February

I wondered how it had come to this.

No. That wasn't right.

I knew exactly how it had come to this.

Lightning shattered the sky and raked the black surface of the ocean. The rain spilling out from above hit my face and body like a shower as I stood on my patio, soaking me and the duffel bag slung over my shoulder. The water stung the cut above my eye and grew the bloody stain on my shirt.

I knew that I wouldn't ever stand on this patio again, stare at this view again, live in this home again.

Thunder rolled off the Pacific like it was coming through a megaphone, rattling the windows and doors of all the homes on the boardwalk. The rain picked up velocity, splashing into the puddles on the ground.

I wiped the water from my eyes and took another look, making sure that all of it—my home, the view, this world I had created for myself— would never leave my memory.

I knew that it wouldn't. And I knew that the memories of the last month wouldn't leave me either.

Things like that don't leave you. They inhabit you. Forever.

I turned to the glass door and squinted through the reflected bands of rain. My gun lay on the kitchen table. Two surfboards stood in the corner. Most everything I owned was still inside. I didn't know what would happen to those things. And I didn't care.

The lightning cracked again behind me. A starter's pistol, telling me it was time to go.

I stepped off the patio and headed for the car, leaving the remains of my life behind.

WEEK ONE

ONE

"You have an admirer," Liz Santangelo said.

She and I were on my patio under a San Diego sun that was threatening to disappear into a February storm. I was getting ready to hit the water, and Liz was about to head to work.

Without turning to look, I knew who she meant. A woman in her late twenties, small, attractive. She'd bicycled past on the board-walk when Liz and I had first stepped outside. Now she was on the beach, off to our right, pretending to read a book. She was trying to be unobtrusive. I wasn't the world's greatest PI but I knew when someone was keeping an eye on me.

I tied a knot in the drawstring to my board shorts. "I don't have a shirt on. Probably hard for her not to stare."

"She must be too far away to see your faults," Liz replied.

"Bah." I pulled the red rash guard over my head, stretched it over my chest and moved my gaze to the woman. "Just intimidated by my looks."

The woman turned away when our eyes met. She closed her book, picked up her towel, and headed up the beach to the north.

"Yes, clearly she's infatuated," Liz said.

The woman stepped off the sand, crossed the boardwalk, and dis-appeared down one of the many alleys that led to Mission Boulevard. I didn't have an office and people regularly showed up on the beach, as it was the best place to find me. Usually they came and talked to me instead of disappearing into an alley, though.

"A long time ago, you staring at her ass like that would've both-ered me," Liz said, tugging on my hand.

I laughed and turned back to her. "Not what I was looking at."

Liz and I had finally uncomplicated our complicated relation-ship. After years of ebb and flow, we were riding the same current. I was a private investigator; she was a homicide detective. We butted heads professionally, and that had screwed up the personal side of things. But after working a case that made me reevaluate what was important, I had gone looking for some normalcy and good in my life.

I'd found both in Liz.

She glanced up at the sky. "You really going to go surf in the rain?"

"Not raining yet," I said.

"Yet."

February was arguably the worst month of the year in San Diego for weather. It could get downright cold and wet, making the city feel very un-Southern California-like. Watching the thick gray blanket unroll above us on the first day of the month, I thought we might be in for the local version of a monsoon.

I grabbed my board and started keying in the tri-fins. "I can get in a little time before the stinking rain blows it all up."

"Rain is fine," she said, smiling.

"Rain sucks," I said.

She shook her head, but the smile remained.

Things were easy between us. No tension, nothing riding below the surface, no distrust. We'd seen each other at our worst and decided that wasn't so bad. Our lives were better with the other in it. I was happier than I'd ever been, and it was our relationship that was driving that.

"Oh, look," Liz said. "She's baaack."

I got the last fin in place and looked down the boardwalk. The woman had returned, this time with a longboard tucked under her arm. She had replaced her T-shirt with a rash guard. She glanced our way and let her eyes sweep past us, like she was just taking a look up the beach. She walked toward the edge of the water.

"Maybe she wants lessons," Liz suggested, her tone somewhere between amused and annoyed.

I stood. "My day is made."

"How's that?"

"Jealousy. It always makes my day."

Liz rolled her eyes. "I'm not jealous."

"Said the really jealous woman."

She tried to hold in a laugh but failed. "Whatever. I'm leaving."

I leaned over and kissed her. I started to pull away, but she caught my arm and held me there for a moment longer before letting me go.

"Tell her I have a gun and I'm more than happy to use it," she said.

I watched Liz head around the side of the house before turning back to the water. The woman was strapping the leash onto her ankle, surveying the ocean in front of her. Maybe we had overestimated her interest in me, our suspicious natures getting the better of us.

Time to go find out.

TWO

I staked out a spot near the jetty, where the nice right break that sometimes appeared had failed to materialize. The imposing clouds to the west had yet to kick up the larger than normal swells that winter storms brought.

The woman was wearing a bright yellow rash guard and a pair of black bikini bottoms. She had her blond hair pulled back. The board was a little oversized for her, but she handled it okay, paddling into a couple of the small ripples she mistook for waves.

She pretended like she was watching the horizon, waiting for the water to rise up in more respectable swells, but I caught her looking in my direction twice before she finally turned parallel to the shore and paddled over.

"Not so good, huh?" she asked, as she glided up next to me. "I was hoping there'd be a little more going on out here."

"Not in the middle of the day," I said. "Usually just like this."

"Really?" She wrinkled her nose. Her tone was overly friendly. "I was told South Mission was a pretty good spot."

"It can be. Just gotta catch it at the right time."

She nodded like that made sense to her.

"How long are we gonna make the stupid small talk?" I asked.

Her gray eyes shifted away from me, and she pushed a few wet strands of hair off her forehead. "What?"

"You practically camped out on my patio for the last hour," I said. "I saw you walking the beach before you even got in the water." I nodded at her board. "You rented that at Hamel's. And you just told me you've never been out here before."

Thin lines formed above her eyes as she thought about objecting. Then she shrugged. "Got me." She held out a hand. "I'm Darcy Gill."

I didn't shake her hand. "What do you want, Darcy Gill?"

"Nice to meet you, too, Noah Braddock." Her eyes flickered, and the polite friendliness she had brought over with her disappeared as she retracted her hand. "Everyone on the beach said you'd be pissed off if I bothered you on the water."

"They were right."

"But I wasn't sure you'd speak to me if I just showed up at your door," she said. "So I'm sorry for ambushing you like this."

"Sorry enough to just paddle away?" I asked.

"No," she said. "Not that sorry."

"Didn't think so."

"I'm a lawyer," Darcy said.

"Congratulations."

"You're a private investigator, correct?"

"Yep. But I'm not for hire."

"Why not?"

I dipped my hands into the water and then ran them along my arms, goose bumps forming on my skin. I thought about throwing out all my reasons, but she hadn't done anything to earn that knowledge. "Because I'm surfing at the moment."

She stared hard at me for a moment, the intensity of her eyes matching the looming clouds above us. Then she made a face like she didn't care. "That's fine."

"Now will you swim away?"

"In a minute," Darcy said. "If you'll answer one question for me."

"One question and you'll leave me alone?"

"One question."

I didn't believe her, but I wasn't sure what else to do. "Alright."

"How do you feel about the death penalty?" she asked.

I looked at her like she'd grown a dorsal fin. "Excuse me?"

"You heard me."

I squinted into the blue-gray sky to the west. "That's your one question?"

"Yeah."

I laughed, then shrugged. "Okay. I'm in favor of it. Goodbye, Darcy Gill."

"Why are you in favor of it?" she asked.

"No, no. That's two questions."

"Come on," she said. "You already told me you aren't for hire. Just answer me."

I resented her interrupting my quiet afternoon, but I wasn't ready to get off the water yet. And drowning her would have been too obvious.

"Fine," I said. "I support the death penalty because I believe that there are some people who simply don't belong on the planet. They aren't here to do anything other than damage the world."

"I agree that some people aren't fit for this world," she said, "but it doesn't mean killing a person is correct."

"No, it doesn't," I said. "But that's the way the world works, and that's my opinion."

"I have a client on death row," she said. "His execution date is in a month."

"I'm sorry to hear that," I said, watching the water spill off the jetty. "But I'm gonna assume that your client may have done something that justified his current position."

"He did," she said. "He killed two other men."

"There you go."

"The problem for me, Mr. Braddock, is that my client won't talk to me," she said. "He's willing to accept the punishment. But I'm not."

"Isn't that his choice?" I said.

"Maybe," she answered. "But I don't believe in the death penalty, and it's my job to see if I can change his sentence."

I sat there, the last of the sun beating down on my shoulders, knowing there was more to this conversation.

"You said you didn't care that I wasn't for hire," I said.

"I lied," she said, smiling, exposing a slight gap between her two front teeth.

"Then you've wasted your time," I said as I lay down on the board.

"I think I can change your mind," she said.

I started paddling in. "Then you're wrong."

I heard her thrashing in the water behind me, her small arms working furiously to catch up to me. I stroked hard until my fingers grazed the sand below the water.

"You haven't asked me about my client," she said, catching me sooner than I'd anticipated.

"Sharp observation, Darcy." I stopped paddling, slid off the board, and stood next to it, maybe twenty yards from the sand, the water just below my knees. "I'm not interested."

She pushed off her board, fell awkwardly into the water, then bounced up to her feet. She shoved her rental angrily toward the shore and put her hands on her hips. "Ask me who my client is."

I put a finger to my chin like I was thinking, then pulled it away. "No."

"I'm not going away until you ask," she said.

She had the feel of someone who would back that statement up, nipping at my heels as I tried to kick her away.

"Christ," I said, reaching down to my ankle and unstrapping the leash. "If I ask, will you go the fuck away?"

"Yeah."

"Even when I tell you that I'm still not interested? You'll go away and no more of this shit?"

"I promise," she said.

"I heard that once already."

"This time I mean it," she said. "If you want me to go away, I'll go away."

There was something in her demeanor that suddenly made me realize I didn't want to ask the question. She seemed supremely confident.

But I was stuck.

"Who is your client?" I asked.

"My client is Russell Simington," she said.

The name meant absolutely nothing to me. "So?"

Darcy Gill folded her arms across her chest, casting a long, thin shadow across the shallow water. "Russell Simington is your father."

THREE

I walked out of the ocean, the board tucked under my arm and Darcy Gill chasing behind me.

"Did you hear me?" she asked, coming up to my side.

"I heard you."

"Your father is on death row."

"I don't have a father," I said.

"Spare me the Movie of the Week drama," she said, keeping pace. "I know you don't have a relationship with him. But he is still your father."

I trudged up the sand, stepped across the pavement of the board-walk, and set my board down behind the small retaining wall that bordered my patio.

I turned to Darcy. "I didn't even know his name until you just said it. I don't know that this guy is my father."

"Your mother is Carolina, correct?" she said, dropping her rental board against the wall.

I didn't say anything.

"He told me where to find you," she said. "He told me who your mother is. I checked you out. He got your birth date correct. He is your father, whether you want to believe me or not. And he is scheduled to die."

The temperature was in the high sixties, but I fought off a shiver.

I sat down on the wall. "He knew where to find me?"

Darcy nodded. "He knew your address by memory. And your mother's." She paused. "And you would have no way of knowing this, but you look a hell of a lot like him."

Something lurched in my gut. I'd never known a thing about my father. Knowing my mother had nearly done me in. She'd never brought him up, and I'd never asked. There were veiled references on occasion, but nothing strong enough to start a conversation. I'd done fine without a father and, over the years, that independence had only grown stronger and quashed any fleeting curiosity I might have had in learning anything about him.

"Who did he kill?" I asked, trying to get my thoughts in order.

"Two Mexican nationals," she said, sitting down next to me. "Five years ago. He shot them point blank in the back of the head, hands tied behind their backs."

"Sounds like a guy I really want to meet."

"Look, I'm not going to lie to you," she said. "You can find out the facts pretty easily, so there's no point in it. He's a hard man. He's comfortable in jail. He'd been in before this conviction."

I didn't know how to feel about that. On one hand, it didn't matter. I'd never met him, never spoken to him, and never touched him. The only influence he'd had on my life was my having to give an embarrassing answer when people asked where my father was.

On the other hand, if he was truly my father, the blood of a lifelong criminal was pulsing in my heart.

"He was convicted with special circumstances that allowed for the death penalty," Darcy continued. "He's never participated in his appeals, and he's waived the opportunity for several of them even to be heard. That's why he's come up so fast. He's been on the row for eighteen months. Generally, the average is thirteen years before we get to this point."

"Why hasn't he appealed?"

"I don't know," she said. "I just picked up this case last month. I work for a firm that only handles appellate cases. We grab cases like your father's."

"Don't call him that," I said sharply. "And I know what appellate firms do."

"Then you know we're his last chance," she said. "The attorneys who handled his earlier appeals told me that he just wasn't interested in spending time in court anymore. He's barely spoken to me."

I stared at the gray sky draping the ocean like a big canopy. "Why would you think I'd give a shit about helping him?"

"I don't. But you're basically my last option to get him to talk."

"Talk about what?"

She shuffled her feet on the concrete walk. "He killed those two men. There's no doubt about that, and he confessed to it. But when he was first arrested, he indicated that he was working for someone. He's denied it ever since. But if I can show that he was under orders, it might buy him a little sympathy and get the sentence commuted to life."

"You already told me he's not talking."

"Not to me. But he might to you."

I couldn't imagine what he'd have to say to me. And I'd reached a point in my life where I didn't think I really had anything to say to him. Not anything that was worth the anger it would bring to the surface, anyway.

"Why would he talk to me?" I asked. "We don't know each other."

"The only words he's said to me were about you," she said. "Coming from a man facing a death sentence, that says a great deal about where his mind and heart are."

I feared she was right.

FOUR

"You said Simington might have been working for someone," I said, folding my arms across my chest. "You know that for sure?"

Darcy shook her head. "Not for sure, no. But looking at his history, Simington's never been a leader. His record shows that he's always been a middle man. A guy who takes orders."

"What else has he done time for?"

"Armed robbery, assault, and various weapons charges. He did five years on the robbery and less than a year each on the others. Walked on several other charges."

A bank of clouds moved in front of the sun and shaded the beach. The shadows added to the sour feeling in my stomach.

"Any idea who he was working for?" I asked.

"Not really," she replied. "But I found a pattern in his employment. For the previous three years until his final arrest, he was working as a security guard for some different casinos."

Putting a convicted felon in a casino was enough to raise anyone's eyebrows.

"Any explanation for the murders?"

"None that Simington would give," she said. "The detectives that put his case together tied him to an alien smuggling ring, but he never confirmed. Or denied."

"Alien smuggling. You think Simington helped bring Mexicans across the border?"

She fixed me with her gray eyes. "Yes. I'm not sure exactly what his role was, but I believe Russell Simington—your father—was involved with that."

I forced my mouth to keep from asking another question. I hated the fact that I was already curious, wanting to know more about Russell Simington. I didn't want to want any part of this, and yet, I was already feeling a gravitational pull.

"Look, I know this will be difficult for you," Darcy said.

"*Will* be difficult?" I said, equally amused and annoyed. "When did I say yes? Did I miss it?"

She pursed her lips, accepting the chastisement. "I understand that you never knew him. But I'm not asking you to develop a relationship with him."

"That's exactly what you're asking," I said. "The moment I look at him, it becomes a relationship."

She pulled at the yellow rash guard as if the neoprene T-shirt was too tight. Her intensity was almost tangible, like a force field around her.

"I don't believe in the death penalty," she finally said. "It's wrong. I decided a long time ago that I would commit my life to stopping it. I don't apologize for that. But I can't control who it brings me to or whose lives I have to disrupt in order to stop it." The first bank of clouds passed, and the sun splintered through. "This time, it's brought me to you."

"Lucky fucking me."

"Just go talk to him," she said, leaning closer. "Just once. If he won't talk to you or it gets ugly, fine. You're out, and I won't bother you again." She leaned back and shrugged. "I'll figure out another way to get his story, and I won't involve you."

"How about not involving me now?" I said. "Or for that matter, ever? I don't recall any of this being on my Christmas wish list."

She shook her head and looked away, not appreciating the remark.

The ocean was dying as the storm trudged in, going flat with thin lines of white foam trickling in to the shore. We stood there for a few moments, not saying anything. We both knew she was getting to me, yet I wasn't willing to acknowledge it and she seemed content to wait me out.

"Where is he?" I asked.

"San Quentin," she said. Her cheeks were bright pink, a combination of sunburn and emotion. "It's the only place in California that houses male death row inmates."

"Do I just show up?" I asked. "Knock on the door and ask when visiting hours are?"

"I've already set up a visitation time," she said. "I've booked a flight that leaves for San Francisco the day after tomorrow. For both of us."

I laughed and shook my head at her bravado. "At least you're confident."

She rose from the wall and stood in front of me, the muscles in her jaw tense. "I told you his execution date is a month away. Twenty-seven days. I can't afford to waste time. Because it's his time I'd be wasting."

I wanted to tell her that all of this was going to be a waste of time—that, no matter what, I wasn't about to overlook all of the years this man had already pissed away. I may have been able to overlook the void in my life growing up, but it didn't mean that I appreciated it, forgave it, or would ever accept it. Those feelings were bound to come out in any conversation with him. His death would just add finality to the void that had been a partner in my life.

I stood. "I'll think about it."

Her face screwed up with irritation. "I just told you I had the visitation set up."

"Yes, you did. Congratulations."

"We can't afford to waste time."

"You explained that, too." I ignored the "we" and stepped over the wall onto my patio. "You've been aggravatingly thorough."

Darcy stood on the boardwalk, the small wall between us seeming more like a gigantic barrier now. She picked up the rental board, clearly agitated.

"The flight leaves at nine," she said, her voice edged with frustration and anger. "How will I know if you're coming?"

I glanced at her. "Are the seats on the plane together?"

She brushed her wet, blond hair off her forehead and glared at me. "Yeah. Of course."

"Then check the seat next to yours," I said to Darcy Gill. "That'll give you your answer."

FIVE

I showered, dressed, made a sandwich, and sat down in front of the TV with a beer to watch the second half of the San Diego State/UCLA basketball game. The Aztecs were starting to turn things around in the hoops program, and I was hoping the game would keep thoughts of Darcy Gill and Russell Simington out of my head.

The Aztecs were up by six when Carter bounded in the front door.

"Are you watching this?" he yelled as he hustled past me into the kitchen. "Gonna beat those Westwood weasels for the first time in forever."

"Easy. Don't jinx it."

He jumped over the back of the couch and landed with a thud, two beers in one huge hand. "Done deal, baby."

"Get a beer, why don't you?"

He held one up to his mouth and emptied half of it, then let loose with a belch that rattled the windows. "Thanks. I think I'll have two." He was wearing a green tank top, red board shorts, and yellow flip-flops that matched the color of his hair. "I thought you were coming over to my place to watch this."

"Forgot."

"You forgot?"

I grunted in response.

The Aztecs threw the ball away four times in the last two minutes, which elicited a stream of profanity from Carter that would have cleared a locker room. But they managed to hit several free throws and hung on to win by four.

Carter stood, arms raised over his head, his fingers touching the ceiling. "I love beating those assholes."

I walked into the kitchen and set my plate and empty beer bottle on the counter. "You on the team now? A uniform and everything?"

He brought his bottles to the kitchen. "Here's a question. What the fuck is up your ass today?"

I dropped the bottles into the trash can beneath the sink. "Nothing."

"Nothing is what a fat man leaves on his plate and what the ladies are yearning for when I'm done with them. But it is most definitely not what is bothering you."

"That makes no sense."

He waved a hand in the air. "Fuck off. You know what I mean."

I did, but I wasn't sure how to explain what was rattling around in my head.

I leaned on the counter. "Have I ever mentioned my father to you?"

His features softened, and he slid into a chair at the dining room table. "No, I don't think so."

That alone said so much about our friendship. I'd known Carter for fifteen years, and not once had he ever asked about my father. Not a single question. Somewhere along the road, he'd recognized that it wasn't a subject I was comfortable talking about and he'd left it to me to broach the subject. He'd shown an enormous amount of patience.

"I don't really know anything about him," I said.

Carter shrugged. "I figured."

"I mean, like nothing. No name, no location, nothing."

He didn't say anything, his face devoid of expression.

"Never really gave a shit, you know?" I said. "I had enough going on with Carolina. It was just the two of us, and I thought I didn't miss what I didn't have."

Carter shifted in the chair and gave a slight nod.

"Figured if I ever ran into him, I'd just beat the shit out of him anyway, so it was better to not even bother."

"Sounds about right."

I flicked a stray bottle cap off the counter and into the sink. "So this woman shows up today

"What woman?"

"Just a woman who showed up while I was on the water."

"Was she hot?"

I frowned at him. "Would you let me finish?"

"Okay."

"She said she knows my father."

He propped his elbow on the table and put his lantern-like jaw in his hand. "You believe her?"

"Think so."

"How does she know him?"

The insecurities that had plagued me for a lifetime came awake, and I couldn't give him a completely truthful answer.

"It's complicated," I said.

Carter didn't miss a beat, letting me slide. "He wants to meet you?"

"Yeah. I guess that's what it is."

"What did you tell her?"

"Said I'd let her know."

"And I assume you're working on that?"

"All day." I hesitated. "I have no idea what to do."

He laughed. "You asking me for advice, Noah?"

"I don't know what the hell I'm asking. But I guess I want your opinion."

"First off, I'm not exactly a great candidate for this question," he said, raising an eyebrow. "You know how I feel about my father."

I did. He didn't care for him. L. Martin Hamm was a Marine who failed miserably in trying to install Marine Corps discipline in his son. He'd taken that failure personally, declared his son a waste, and moved with Carter's mother to Florida a week after Carter had finished high school. As far as I knew, they hadn't spoken since.

"And I'm not sure my opinion will mean anything," he said.

"Why not?"

"I've never been in your situation," he said. "Master Sergeant Hamm and I never got along, but he was always a presence when I was growing up. Like him or not, he was there. I didn't have a choice in knowing him. You, it seems, have a choice."

I nodded and stared out the kitchen window at the water. Choice was supposed to be a good thing, but I wasn't buying it at the moment.

"That said, I'd think that if you believe this chick, then not meeting him might eat you up for a while," he said. "Knowing that he really does exist."

That exact idea had already worked me over since Darcy had announced her reasons for visiting me. "I know."

"Nothing says you can't beat the shit out of him when you meet him. You're entitled."

I figured the prison officials might see it differently, but didn't say so.

"Are you curious?" he asked.

Anxiety pounded away in my gut. "Yeah. More than I want to be. But, yeah, I am."

"Then just do it," he said. "You don't owe him anything. Don't do it for him or for this chick. Do it for you. You can look him in the eye and walk away. It doesn't have to be anything more than you want it to be. But don't let it drive you crazy wondering."

He was right, which wasn't unusual. He knew me better than anyone and he was always honest with me. I valued that honesty, even if I didn't always want to hear it. He saw things in me that I couldn't or maybe didn't want to see.

So I hated not telling Carter that there was more to be curious about than just this man's identity. I felt guilty for initiating the conversation and only sharing half the story. But I wasn't ready to pull the curtain all the way back on my life, even to my best friend.

Carter stood. "I think I'd wanna meet him. If it were me."

"Why?"

"So he'd know that I knew who he was. So I could stand there, stare at him, and make him uncomfortable. I probably wouldn't even say a word to him." He paused, his intense, dark eyes fixing on me. "But I'm not you."

He didn't know how lucky he was.

SIX

I spent the next day poking around on the computer and at the library. Found some news articles on Russell Simington, but no photos. Nothing earth-shattering, but nothing that made me want to meet him either. As I was looking at those articles, I was also scanning my brain for any recall of my father. I came up empty and no closer to making a decision as to whether I'd join Darcy on the plane the following morning.

I didn't disagree with anything Carter had suggested. It would eat away at me if I missed the opportunity to meet my father. But I'd gone nearly thirty years without knowing who the man was, and I felt like I'd done okay so far. Maybe I was kidding myself, though.

When I left the library, the sun was starting to move behind the water, the rain lying in wait. My time to make a decision was disappearing fast.

And I was going to be late for a date.

I went home and changed into a pair of khaki shorts and a Quiksilver button-down shirt and headed out into the evening.

I had the windows down in the Jeep as I drove south toward downtown. The remains of the day had receded into the dusky sky, leaving the air feeling crisp and clean. The sun was exploding into a kaleidoscope of purples and oranges to the west, flashing brightly as the ocean pulled it downward. I exited the freeway and curved around Lindbergh Field, not envying the pilots who had to land their planes while looking into the blinding sunset.

I went past the airport entrance and onto Harbor Island. The mile and a half long island had been created by the navy in the early 1960s when they dredged San Diego Bay to make it deep enough for the military ships arriving in port. The navy took the mud and sand from the bottom of the bay and turned it into this narrow strip of land that housed upscale hotels, restaurants, and marinas. Tom Ham's Lighthouse, a seafood restaurant, sat at the western edge of the island, and I pulled into the parking lot.

Liz was waiting out front.

She wore black walking shorts, black sandals, and a sleeveless white blouse, exposing her olive skin. She pushed her sunglasses up off her face into her mane of raven hair, her smile reaching her bright blue eyes. She held up a hand and waved.

I tried not to trip.

"I was starting to wonder if you'd forgotten me," she said. "Maybe run away with that little surfer girl from yesterday."

I kissed her. She smelled like strawberries and mint and everything else good. "Not ever."

Her hand slid into mine. "Suck up."

"Not ever."

Her smile broadened, sending a shot of electricity through me, and we strolled into the restaurant.

We were shown to a small table along the window with a view of the city skyline and the boats bobbing in the harbor. Liz ordered a Cosmopolitan, and I asked for a Jack and Coke.

She gazed at me across the table as we waited for our drinks. "You look tired."

I folded my hands on the table and took a deep breath. "I am."

"Were you in the water all day?"

"Actually, not at all today. Not much happening. I think the threat of rain smothered the swells."

She tilted her head to the side. "Is that even possible?"

"No. But it sounds good."

Our drinks arrived, and I emptied half of mine before setting it down.

"How was your day?" I asked.

She made a face like I'd dropped a skunk on the table. "Shitty. Picked up two new cases that we don't have the time for. John's ready to quit."

John Wellton was her partner in the homicide department. The city's annual mismanagement of funding had resulted in more budget cuts, this time slashing through law enforcement. She and Wellton were doing the work of four teams.

"I'm sorry," I said.

She picked up her menu. "And that's the last I'm saying about work tonight."

"Fine by me."

Our waitress came back, and we ordered. Mahi-mahi for Liz and swordfish for me.

Liz took another sip of her drink and reached across the table for my hand. "Are you going to tell me about your admirer or do I have to pry?"

Being with Liz lifted my spirits, but it couldn't eliminate Darcy's revelation from the previous day.

I squeezed her hand. "I was getting there."

"Okay."

I pulled my hand away and picked up my drink. "You ever run across a case involving a guy named Russell Simington?"

She made a face. "I recall the name. Something about killing illegals."

I glanced at the window. Outside, the lights on the Coronado Bridge were bright against the darkening sky.

"From several years back, I think," she said, swirling the light pink liquid in the glass after she took a sip. "We didn't handle it, though. Riverside or El Centro did. Does that sound right?"

"It does."

She set her glass down. "I assume you heard me say no more work talk tonight."

I smiled at her. "I did."

"Then I'll also assume you have a pretty good reason for bringing this guy up."

I stared into my drink, the ice melting slowly in the alcohol and sugar.

"I think Russell Simington is my father," I said.

We sat there for a few minutes without speaking. Liz's face told me she was working out what to say next. Our food arrived, and the waitress asked if we needed anything else. We both shook our heads.

"Will you explain it to me?" Liz finally asked.

I told her about my conversation with Darcy Gill, ignoring the twinge of guilt I felt for not opening up the same way to Carter. I told her about San Quentin and death row and everything else.

She stuck a fork in her food, then rested it on the plate, distracted. "I can check it out. If you want. See if she's legit."

I shook my head. "I think she's telling the truth. But I'll find out for myself."

She nodded and picked up her fork.

We ate quietly for a few minutes. I knew I'd changed the course and tone of our evening, but I wanted to tell her. It was the kind of thing I would have kept from her in the past.

"He was a bad guy," she said.

"Figured."

"No, I mean *bad*," she repeated. "If I'm remembering correctly, the way it went down, it was ugly."

Her conviction was like a kick in the groin. "That's the impression I got from this lawyer."

She bunched up her napkin and laid it on the table next to her plate. "Are you gonna go?"

I leaned back in the chair. "I haven't decided."

She started to say something, then stopped.

"Say it," I said. "Whatever you were just about to say."

"I think it would be hard, Noah," she said, softly. "Not that you shouldn't do it, but I think it will be tough and you should be ready for that."

"I know. Seeing this guy who's done all these things," I said. "And then realizing that I'm his son. I'm not sure what I get out of it or if I should even want anything out of it."

She nodded. "Yeah, I think you should consider all those things. But I was looking at it a little differently."

"What do you mean?"

The waitress came and cleared the table, and we passed on dessert.

Liz put her elbows on the table and leaned forward. "Let's say you go and meet with him. You learning anything that might enable this woman to get him off death row is really unlikely. In California, once they punch your ticket for the chamber, it's a done deal. He's probably going to die regardless of what he may tell you."

"I know that. And it sounds like he deserves to," I said.

She shook her head and pushed a stray strand of hair away from her face. "You're assuming that he's going to be this awful person, this guy who matches the image you've created of him. What if he's not like that at all?"

"I'm not following you."

She stared at me, her blue eyes radiating concern. "What if you like him?"

Silverware clinked against plates and murmured conversation drifted in the air around us.

"I'm not saying I don't want you to do this," she said, reaching across the table and taking my hand. "I'm really not. You probably need to do it. But you're talking about him as if you've already met him and you know exactly how he's going to be." She paused. "You need to consider the idea that he's not going to be a monster and that you may feel some connection to him. And that might be hard to deal with when the time comes for him to die."

Her words felt like a slap to the side of my head. She was right. I hadn't thought of it that way. The indecision and fear I'd been fighting all day went up a notch.

She laced her fingers with mine and squeezed my hand. "I'll help any way I can. But are you ready for all those possibilities?"

I appreciated her asking, but we both knew I wasn't.

SEVEN

We spent the night at my place, and I was awake at four in the morning, staring at the ceiling, knowing I was going to the airport.

I didn't pack a bag. I wasn't planning on staying longer than the afternoon.

I woke Liz after I showered and told her I'd call her later on. She hugged me, maybe a moment or two longer than usual, then kissed me goodbye without saying a word.

The drive to Lindbergh took twenty minutes on the empty freeway, and I was ticketed and through security by seven thirty. I didn't feel like talking with Darcy until I had to, so I bought a paper and sat down with it in the coffee shop to have some breakfast.

Neither the paper nor the greasy eggs were able to keep my mind off what I was venturing into. I wasn't sure I'd be able to balance what Darcy wanted me to find out and what I needed to know for myself. I didn't think that Simington would have given her my information just so he could tell me the entire truth about his crime. I had a feeling it had more to do with making amends before his death.

I watched people walk to their gates and questions kept popping into my head. Did I really look like his son? How would he introduce himself? What was it like inside San Quentin? Would he have excuses for his actions or would he take pride in what he'd done?

I wasn't sure I wanted answers to any of those questions, but I knew I was getting on that plane.

The first boarding call went out over the loudspeaker, and my stomach tightened.

At eight fifteen, I figured I couldn't postpone the inevitable as they made the last call for passengers to San Francisco.

I walked through the Jetway, my stomach already churning. I was carrying self-doubt and second guesses like pennies in my pocket.

The cabin was three-quarters full. Business travelers in suits. Some college-aged kids. A mother with a small child strapped to her body in the first row. She smiled at me as I went by, and I returned her smile.

My ticket said 10C.

I worked my way up the aisle and reached row ten. D, E, and F were occupied by two teenagers and a guy reading the *Wall Street Journal*. A guy reading the *New York Times* was in A, next to the window.

B was empty.

Darcy Gill was nowhere to be found.

I slid into my seat and glanced around. I didn't see her. I wondered if she'd taken a flight the previous night, our conversation on the beach convincing her I wouldn't be joining her. Or maybe she was running late.

The doors to the plane closed, we pushed back from the gate, and the attendants began their run-through of the safety procedures.

Darcy didn't strike me as someone who ever ran late.

I was annoyed that I'd gotten up in the dark and boarded a plane at her request and Darcy was a no-show. I wondered momentarily if she was playing some game.

But just as she didn't strike me as someone who showed up tardy, I didn't think Darcy was a game player either.

I glanced at the empty seat next to me.

As the flight attendants took their seats and the plane taxied down the runway for takeoff, the anxious burning that had taken up residence in my gut since Darcy had accosted me in the water gained new life.

EIGHT

The flight was bumpy and rough as the plane navigated the thick marine layer along the coast, and I felt like a ping-pong ball by the time we landed.

I wasn't sure what I was supposed to do. Darcy was supposed to be my tour guide.

I dialed information on my cell and asked for a number for Darcy Gill. Information had a business number for her at a law firm called Gill and Gill. When I was connected, I heard a recording giving some perfunctory information. One of those pieces of information was Gill and Gill's address.

I walked outside and jumped in a taxi. I gave the driver the address, and we moved away from the congestion of the airport.

San Francisco had never been my favorite place. Cold, rainy, and carrying an inferiority complex that it constantly denied, the city never felt like it belonged in California. The views were spectacular across the bays and the Golden Gate was pretty enough, but the place never felt comfortable.

A missing Darcy and a meeting with Russell Simington had taken that uncomfortability to new heights.

The taxi driver, a small Asian man who didn't speak a word to me, navigated the streets of the city with the care of a wounded bull. The plane ride was nothing compared to the lightning-quick lane changes, rocket-like acceleration, and indifference toward red lights.

The taxi pulled up to a three-story building that appeared to be waiting for a breeze to knock it over. The drywall on the outside was chipped away, a window on the top floor was boarded up, and the wooden door looked about two hundred years old. A small sign next to the door read "Gill and Gill." Law firm, crack house. Same difference.

I paid the silent man his money and stepped out into the wet, heavy morning air. The taxi exploded away from the curb, its tires screeching on the damp pavement.

I pushed open the old wooden door. I was in a short, low-ceilinged hallway book-ended by another door at the opposite end. A frosted glass pane in the middle of the door had "Law Offices" stenciled on it.

I opened that door into a room the size of a Geo Metro. A young woman looked up at me from behind a cluttered desk. Her hair was dyed jet black, with a purple streak right through the center. Each ear held a multitude of earrings. Her eyes were heavily lined with eyeliner and mascara, and her lipstick was nearly as dark. Her pale skin seemed to glow against the hair and makeup.

"Can I help you?" she asked, sounding like she didn't want to.

"I'm looking for Darcy Gill."

"She's not in," she said.

"Know where I can find her?"

"No. I wish I did," she said, annoyed.

"Is she still in San Diego?" I asked.

Surprise and curiosity appeared on her face. "I don't know. Who are you?"

"Noah Braddock. She came to see me yesterday."

She stood up. She wore a long-sleeved black sweater and black jeans that looked too big for her skinny frame. She looked me over like she was seeing me for the first time.

"She's not with you?" she said, her voice now sounding like she cared.

"She was supposed to meet me on the plane. I was on it. She wasn't."

She stared hard at me for a moment, her eyes cold and unfriendly.

"Shit," she said.

"Who are you?" I asked.

"Miranda," she said, her eyes on her desk now, thinking. "I'm her paralegal."

"Who's the other Gill in the firm?"

"There isn't one. Darcy thought it sounded better than just her name."

"Ah."

"When did you last talk to her?"

I recounted our conversation on the beach.

"And she was gonna meet you at the airport, right?"

"She said she'd be on the plane. I told her I wasn't sure what I was doing."

Miranda nodded. "Yeah. I talked to her right after that. She said you were kind of a dick."

"I'll be sure to ask her about that. So she didn't come back last night?"

"If she did, I haven't talked to her," she said. "But she had reservations on the morning flight. I left a couple of messages on her cell, but she never called back."

It didn't feel right. Darcy had come down to San Diego for one reason—getting me to San Francisco. It made no sense that she would miss the flight. If anything, I had half expected her to show up at my house and escort me to the airport.

"Do you know where she was staying?" I asked.

"Yeah," Miranda said. "I need to make a couple of calls. She may have just got caught up with something else." She pointed a finger at me. Her nails were black. Shocker. "And you need to get over to Quentin to see your dad."

I bristled. "His name is Russell Simington, and I don't know that he's related to me."

She held up her hands in mock apology. "Right, dude. Sorry. Not like you don't look just like him or anything."

Darcy had said the same thing, and I didn't feel any better hearing it a second time. "You've seen him?"

"Of course. It's the only thing we're doing now."

"You and Darcy are the whole office?"

Miranda started looking through the papers on her desk. "The whole office."

"And you're a paralegal?"

She snorted. "That's my title. I'm third year at Hastings. Secretary, paralegal, investigator, office manager. I do it all." She pulled a piece of paper from a stack. "Here we go. Eleven thirty is check-in."

"For what?"

"Visiting hours start at noon," she said. "You need to be there at eleven thirty so they can check your ID, do the cavity search, all that stuff."

Miranda thought she was funny. I thought different.

She shoved the paper in my direction. "Fill this out before you get there. They'll want it from you at the gate."

I took the paper. "What about Darcy?"

The corners of her mouth flashed into a little smile. "You need someone to hold your hand?"

"No. I meant what are you going to do to find her?"

"It's a scary place over there," she said, still smiling. "All those mean, nasty men. I could get my sister to go with you. She's thirteen, but she's tough."

"You treat all your clients like this?"

"Other than Russell, we don't have any clients right now," she said, the smile fading.

"Imagine."

She waved a hand in the air. "Go. They won't let you in if you're late. I'll work on tracking down Darcy."

"Maybe your sister can help you out," I said, turning to leave.

"Hey," Miranda called out. "Noah?"

I opened the door. "What?"

"Say hi to your daddy."

I slammed the door behind me.

NINE

Two blocks away from Miranda, I waved down a taxi. I didn't know where Darcy was, but I had other things to worry about.

The cab went north out of the city. The irony was that California's most violent prison sat on a beautiful plateau next to San Francisco Bay in one of the wealthiest counties in the state. For years there had been rumors that the state would sell the land to developers for billions and ship the prisoners to other prisons. But, so far, they remained incarcerated with an ocean view.

I looked at the paperwork Miranda had given me. Basic stuff about who I was and why I was visiting. Probably just to have a record of me in case I tried to break someone out.

Not likely.

The cab pulled to a halt outside the entrance.

The driver turned around. "This is as far as I go. Bad luck to drive in there."

I handed him the fare and tip. "Probably bad luck to walk in, too."

"No doubt, man."

The front of the prison looked like a city park. Big grassy lawns with palm trees. The parking lot was full, and there was a line at the main gate. A knot like a rock formed in my stomach as I got in line.

The guard greeted me with a big smile. She looked at my paperwork, nodded, asked me a few routine questions. She handed back my license, but kept the paperwork. "You'll have exactly fifty minutes, sir. We'll notify you when there are ten minutes left." She upped the wattage in the smile. "Welcome to San Quentin."

I walked through a metal detector and into an expansive courtyard. People talked casually, the prisoners identified by their bright yellow coveralls. Babies cried, toddlers ran in circles, and men and women held hands, trying to act like normal families. But the forced smiles and reserved actions told the real story.

I felt like I was entering some sort of deranged amusement park.

A guard explained to me that death row inmates were not allowed into the public areas, and I was directed through another gate and to a bank of windows down a narrow hall.

I didn't argue.

I slid into a seat in front of the last window and my assisting guard told me that Mr. Simington would be along shortly. In the center of the window was a small circle with slats running through it, like in the box office of a movie theater.

Only this movie was real.

Sitting there by myself, the urge to run was greater than anything I'd ever felt. I had no place being there. I could live without meeting this man. My life would be no different. I owed nothing to him or to Darcy Gill. Nothing. Going through with this suddenly seemed like a ridiculous exercise in masochism, and I stood to get the hell out of there.

There was movement behind the window and a guard pulled back the chair on the other side of the clear panel.

I froze.

Run or sit?

I sat.

The guard moved away, and Russell Simington moved into view.

He was a little over six feet tall and well built, the yellow coveralls fitting him like a tailored business suit. I put him somewhere in his late fifties. Thick brown hair streaked with gray. The reading glasses he wore over his dark green eyes gave him an educated look. A nondescript nose. His skin was darker than I expected for someone in his position, a golden brown that only the sun can give. A tiny white scar stood out next to his right eye. A well-manicured beard, brown with gray like his hair, covered a distinguished jaw line. I saw a small tattoo near his right wrist, but I couldn't make it out.

I felt my breath getting away from me.

If Russell Simington wasn't my father, someone had done a damn good job of drawing us with the same pencil.

He slid into the chair and gave a slight nod in my direction.

"Hello," he said. His voice was deep but smooth.

"Hi," I managed.

He leaned forward, his face closer to the panel, and adjusted his glasses. "I'm Russell."

I said nothing.

"And unless I'm looking in some sort of trick mirror that takes me back a ways, you must be Noah." A small, tired smile emerged on his mouth.

I shifted in the chair. "Yeah. I'm Noah."

He folded his hands on the small ledge below the panel. "It's nice for me to meet you, but I expect it's not the same for you."

"Not exactly."

He nodded as if that was the response he expected. "I assume you're here because that Darcy woman found you."

My heart was thumping, almost as if it was beating against my ribcage. "Yeah."

He shook his head, chuckling to himself. "She is a pistol, that one. Surprised she's not here with you, actually."

Even if I could have, I didn't feel the need to explain her absence to him. So I said nothing.

He cleared his throat. "I'm not sure what else we're supposed to do."

"Me either."

"She told you about me?"

"I got all the highlights."

He studied me for a moment, then laughed. "Highlights."

We sat there in silence. It felt like everything I'd expected and nothing I'd expected, all at the same time.

"How is Carolina?" he asked.

"Fine."

"You and she close?"

"None of your fucking business."

He pursed his lips. "I suppose."

Everything seemed to be closing in around me, and I needed to escape.

"Look," I said. "Darcy thinks you'll talk to me and it'll help her win your appeal. Are you going to do that?"

He leaned back in the chair and readjusted the glasses again. "No appeal is going to change my situation. I've done what I've done, and there's no going back." He stared at me with my own eyes. "I'm going to die here, and I'm alright with that."

"Then I am, too," I said quickly.

"As you should be," he said. "But seeing you here, in front of me, has given me some things to think about."

"Good for fucking you."

He came forward again, his hands folded together neatly on the ledge. "I'm not going to fight with you, Noah. All the reasons you hate me are the right ones. I'm not going to try to change that."

He was defusing the anger inside of me, and that made me hate him even more. I wasn't ready to drop thirty years of anger like it was a used napkin. But I was sitting there for a reason, even if I hadn't figured out what it was yet.

"Darcy thinks that you were under orders from someone else to kill," I said, deflecting the conversation away from me. "Were you?"

Russell stared at me, almost through me, his mind elsewhere. Then he snapped back to the present.

"Does it matter?" he asked.

"It might. To her and to your case."

"How about to you?"

I stood. "I'm not here about me and you. I could give a shit about me and you. Darcy is trying to help you. She convinced me to have a conversation with you, so here I am. But I'm not gonna sit here and let you get to know me. I may look like you, but that doesn't mean I am like you."

He sat back in the chair, studying me. It was unnerving.

"You wanna die without fighting, it's fine by me," I said. "You don't wanna give me anything to pass along to Darcy, then I'm outta here."

I felt my chest heaving, and I was furious with myself for getting so worked up. I needed to get it together.

Russell Simington stood up slowly. I saw the tattoo on his wrist clearly now. Small green letters. All capitals. Spelling out my name.

If I could have changed my name on the spot, I would have done it. George, Tom, Mario, whatever. Anything other than what was on his wrist.

"Landon Keene," he said.

I jerked my eyes off the tattoo. "What?"

"Landon Keene," he repeated. "See what you can find out about him." He smiled reluctantly. "You find anything that interests you, then come back and see me. If you want."

Russell Simington disappeared.

TEN

I walked out of San Quentin feeling like I'd just been sprung.

The clouds had lifted, leaving a frosty haze in the sky and a chill in the air.

Or maybe it was me.

A guy across the parking lot watched me as I came out. He made no effort to hide the fact that he had his eyes on me. He was about my height, extra thin, and wore a navy suit that looked too small for him, the pants rising an inch above his shoes and the coat sleeves revealing both wrists. Aviator sunglasses, totally bald.

I took out my cell phone, called the cab company, and heard it would be about ten minutes.

The guy pointed at me and walked in my direction.

I put the phone back in my pocket and waited for him.

"Mr. Braddock," he said as he approached.

"Yeah?"

He pulled out a badge. "Detective Ken Kenney with San Francisco PD."

"Did you just stutter or is that really your name?" I asked.

Kenney smiled, exposing a bunch of crooked teeth. "You have a moment?"

"Not really."

"I think you do," he said, removing his sunglasses.

"Then why'd you ask?"

"Just being polite," he said. He nodded at the prison. "Visiting a friend?"

"No."

"Taking a tour?"

"No. I was getting a manicure."

"Did you visit with Mr. Simington?" His voice was precise, each syllable pronounced.

"Yeah."

"Was he doing well?"

"I didn't ask."

"Ms. Gill asked you to visit him?" Kenney asked.

"Yep."

"But she didn't accompany you?"

"Nope."

He waited for me to elaborate. I didn't.

"Interesting guy, Simington is," Kenney said, twirling his sunglasses by the arm. "You know why he's incarcerated here, correct?"

"Sure. You busted him for parking tickets. You guys take that shit seriously in San Francisco. Well done."

Kenney laughed and stopped the twirling. "Simington was rather humorous, too, from what I recall." He looked at me, the humor gone from his eyes. "Like father like son, I guess."

The blood rushed to my face. "Fuck you."

"Mr. Braddock, we arrested Mr. Simington for a different crime than the one he's currently serving time for. Unfortunately, the case was not prosecuted successfully. Nonetheless, we are very content now that he is residing here, awaiting his punishment." He paused. "We do not wish to see that punishment changed."

"What did you arrest him for?"

"He was hired to kill a young man approximately eight years ago," Kenney said. "He killed the young man in exactly the same manner as the crime he was eventually convicted of."

Russell Simington's past got a little darker and, by default, so did mine.

"So what?" I said. "You think I went in there with a magic wand and commuted his sentence?"

"No, sir," Kenney said, looking at his shoes, then bringing his eyes up slowly to meet mine. "I just want to make it clear that I will do everything in my power to see him remain where he is."

"Good for you."

"I'd hate to have to follow you around the whole time you're visiting San Francisco," Kenney said, with a forced smile, "just to find out what occurred in there."

I sighed, already too tired for so early in the day. "I asked him a few questions. That was it. Darcy wanted some information. He didn't give it to me. And I don't think he ever will."

"I am intrigued that Ms. Gill did not attend with you today," Kenney said, his eyes crinkling as he said it. "That seems atypical of her."

"What can I tell you? Don't know where she is." The cab pulled up outside the main entrance. "My ride's here. See you later."

"Will you be visiting again?" Kenney asked.

"You did a good job of finding out about me this time," I said, smiling at him as I walked away. "Keep on detecting."

ELEVEN

I gave the driver directions back to the offices of Gill and Gill.

The detective's surprise visit rattled me. I was pretty sure he saw it, too. Probably what he was hoping for. I knew that Kenney's case was most likely more complicated than what he had told me. For him to hang on to it like he was doing meant that it had hung on to him.

The cab dropped me off at the same spot outside the old building. Miranda looked more frazzled this time.

"Did she call you?" she asked as I came through the door.

"No. You?"

"No." She gnawed on a black fingernail. "Man, she never goes this long without checking in. And I can't believe she would let you talk to him without being around."

"You know a cop named Kenney?"

She let go of the fingernail. "Yeah. How do you know about him?"

"He was waiting for me when I came out of the prison."

She scowled. "Figures. Even more reason Darcy should've been with you. You tell him anything?"

"Nothing to tell. He was basically just letting me know he doesn't care for Simington."

"He's still pissy about striking out on him years ago," she said. "Probably has front-row reservations for the execution."

"Why?" I asked. "Why does he care so much?"

Miranda sighed. "Simington killed Kenney's nephew. Went ballistic, I guess, when he got off. I wasn't around, but Darcy told me about it."

"Did Simington kill the kid?"

"Definitely," Miranda said. "But the evidence they had was for shit so he skipped. Kenney couldn't work it and Simington did a good enough job covering it up that the cops who did pull it couldn't do a thing with it. Kenney's been sour since."

I was trying to equate the image of a cold-blooded killer with the man I'd just met inside the prison. I was having a hard time getting the two to mesh.

"Kenney's apparently followed his case since he was convicted five years ago. When Simington's number came up on the row a year and a half ago, Kenney made contact with us. He's been by several times to see Darcy, to try to intimidate her and get her to back off, I guess."

"Hard to do," I said.

Miranda's black lips curled into a smile. "She lets him do his thing, talk up all the ways he can end her career and all that. Then when he's done, she opens up the door and waves him out without saying a word." Miranda laughed to herself. "You can almost see his aorta explode."

If Kenney was certain Simington had killed his nephew, I had a hard time blaming him for his stance. Opponents of the death penalty were fond of saying that you can't make the crime personal. The problem was, murder was always personal for someone. Murder left a trail of victims in its wake. In this case, Kenney was one of the victims.

The amusement died on Miranda's face, replaced with concern. "Where the hell is she?"

"I don't know," I said, heading for the door, irritated by the entire situation. "But when you find her, tell her to call me."

"Where are you going?"

"Back to San Diego."

"You're going home?" she asked, incredulous. "You just got here."

"I did what Darcy asked," I said. "She wants to know what he said, she knows where to find me."

TWELVE

My return flight wasn't until the following morning. I tried to change it and was informed it would cost me two hundred bucks, so I spent fifty on a crappy airport motel room instead. I got back to the airport in time for my flight the next morning, my mind swimming with images of Simington's face and voice.

As we descended into San Diego, the clouds were playing tag in the sky, waiting to see which one dropped the first bucket of rain on the ground. I drove to my place, my thoughts bouncing between Darcy, Kenney, and Simington but never coming together to give me an answer about anything.

I shoved my key in my front door to unlock the deadbolt and twisted. There was no resistance, which told me it hadn't been locked to begin with.

I took my hand off the keys, letting them hang in the lock, and listened. If Carter was in there, the TV would be blaring or the stereo rattling the walls.

Nothing.

I walked back to the Jeep, grabbed my gun from beneath the seat, and walked around to the patio off the boardwalk.

The blinds were pulled shut.

I'd lived in that place a long time, since college, because I loved being on the beach and being able to watch the ocean and the sunsets. I could walk to that back slider and gauge the waves every morning or watch the sun slip away each evening.

Not once in all the time I'd lived there had I pulled those blinds shut.

I walked to the front door again. I twisted the knob and swung the door open and stepped to the side, listening.

Quiet.

Dropping to a crouch, I pivoted around the corner into the doorway, my gun leading the way.

Nothing seemed out of place. The sofa was empty, the coffee table as I'd left it. No one in the kitchen or sitting at the dining room table.

I crept in slowly, my ears picking up every tiny sound. I peered down the hallway toward my bedroom. Again, everything seemed normal.

I came up out of the crouch and took a deep breath, my heart rate having spiked. Through the hallway, I could see part of my bed through the open doorway. It hadn't been tossed; it was still made, a habit of Liz's.

I slid next to the sofa to get into the hall and take a more thorough look at my bedroom when something in the area between the back of the sofa and the kitchen caught my eye.

I looked down.

Darcy Gill was lying on my floor, a bullet hole above each eyebrow.

THIRTEEN

Thirty minutes later, an army of cops was wrapping yellow crime scene tape around the perimeter of my place.

I was sure my neighbors would find it charming.

I'd called 911 immediately, then called Liz and told her what I'd walked in on. She put me on hold for a moment, then came back to let me know the responding detectives were already on their way and she'd be there as soon as she could.

Her colleagues found me on the boardwalk.

Harold Klimes looked like a life-size beach ball. Between his neck and his knees, he was a perfect circle of what I guessed to be about three hundred pounds. Not attractive on a guy just under six feet. His pudgy cheeks were bright red and sweat clung to the thinning gray hair above his ears. His eyes looked like tiny targets. He wore a white short-sleeve polyester shirt, a tie that I thought was a clip-on, and gray slacks that barely contained him. A badge was stuck to his belt below the rolls of fat.

I introduced myself, and he stuck out a thick hand. "Hey, Noah." He motioned to my house. "Not good in there, huh?"

I shook his hand, and his grip was what I imagined Superman's to be. "No."

Through the glass slider, I saw several people in coats milling around, staring downward. A camera flashed, no doubt capturing an ugly image of Darcy Gill. I looked away.

Luis Zanella gave me the once-over longer than he needed to before reluctantly holding out his hand. "Hello."

Zanella was a runway model next to Klimes. Brown hair slicked back off a chiseled, tanned face. Alert, green eyes. An expensive-looking pale blue button down open at his neck, exposing a thin, gold chain. Tailored tan slacks that fell to shiny burgundy loafers. Cologne, too much of it, drifted off him. He was a little over six feet with a broad chest and the puffed-out shoulders of a guy who liked looking at himself in the mirror at the gym.

Liz had told me on the phone that Klimes was a good guy and Zanella was a bit of a prick. I thought she was dead on with Klimes but had underestimated his partner.

Zanella lifted his chin at the house. "When did you meet the vic?"

I recounted my meeting with Darcy and my trip to San Francisco again.

Klimes' laugh sounded like he was coughing up a cat. "San Quentin's a fun place, huh?"

"Lots," I said.

"So we should assume this has to do with Simington?" Zanella asked, his eyes moving between me and the house as though he were watching a tennis match.

"Seems like a safe bet. Why else?"

Zanella's eyes zeroed in on me. "Good question. Why else?"

I didn't like his look. "You wanna ask me something, then ask."

He shrugged and the eyes went back to moving.

"No sign of forced entry," Klimes said, dabbing at his sweaty forehead with a handkerchief. "Remember if you had any doors open?"

"Patio might've been unlocked," I said. "Normally is. Liz was here when I left, but I'm sure she locked it behind her. You can check with her."

Klimes nodded. "Makes sense. The tech located blood on the patio near the door."

I glanced in that direction. Two men were hunched over the area, and I couldn't see anything.

"Anybody else's blood on your patio, Mr. Braddock?" Zanella asked.

"Christ, Luis," Klimes said. "Santangelo vouched for him."

Zanella made a face like he didn't know what was what. "Maybe she did that for other reasons."

I'd already had a long day and now Zanella wanted to make it personal, rather than concentrating on the dead woman in my home. I'd had enough.

"How fucking dumb are you?" I asked, stepping in close to him.

I'd caught him off guard, and he took a step back.

"You know I didn't kill her. You know where I was. So that means you're just being an asshole." I leaned closer. "And I don't like assholes, especially ones that smell like they showered in their mothers' perfume."

Zanella's attention was now focused solely on me. He tried to take a step toward me, but I was too close. It was like an awkward hop on his part. And he was pissed.

"I'm running an investigation," he said, the skin around his eyes pinching tight. "You don't like it? Get over it."

"Easy, fellas," Klimes said. "Just cool off."

"And the fact that you are fucking Santangelo doesn't mean shit to me," Zanella said, a little sneer starting to emerge from his lips.

Only the sneer didn't make it all the way onto his face.

My fist got in the way.

FOURTEEN

Zanella toppled over the retaining wall and onto my patio, ripping the yellow tape down with him.

Something hit me with the force of a train, taking me to the pavement and knocking the wind out of me.

There was yelling. I twisted my face as I tried to regain my breath and realized it was Klimes on top of me.

Never underestimate a fat man.

He pulled my arms behind me and slipped cuffs on my wrists. He helped me to my feet.

"Not saying he didn't deserve it," Klimes said, his cheeks bright red. "But you hit my man, and I can't have that." He guided me down the boardwalk two houses down and backed me up to the wall. "Sit here. I'll be back."

I sat. Zanella was just getting up, assisted by two of the uniformed cops. His mouth looked like a child had used a blood-colored crayon to outline it. His eyes were a little unsteady, but he was searching for something. He finally saw me sitting on the wall, and his eyes gained focus. He started for me, but the two cops held onto him and Klimes got in front of him.

"I'm gonna kick your ass!" Zanella yelled, exposing rose-colored teeth.

Liz stepped in front of me before I could respond.

"Well done," she said, shaking her head and removing her sunglasses.

"Maybe the best punch I've ever thrown," I said. "First time I've ever sent anyone over that wall."

"I'll ooh and aah later. What did he say that required you knocking him on his ass?"

"Why don't you ask him?" I said. "I'm not sure if I can remember it exactly.

"Paraphrase."

"He was just being an asshole," I said. "Said something I didn't care for."

She frowned and shook her head. "What a surprise. I told you he was a prick. I didn't mean you could take a swing at him."

I looked away from her. Klimes was talking to Zanella, who was still looking at me. I mouthed "fuck you" at him. His eyes bulged, and he surged forward again. The two uniforms grabbed at him, and Klimes put a hand on his chest.

"Why don't you bring him over so I can apologize?" I said to Liz.

"Funny. I'll be right back."

She walked toward them. Zanella's expression changed, and I could see his dislike for Liz form on his face as she got closer. Made me want to hit him again.

I watched their conversation. Zanella was animated, gesturing in my direction, as he wiped the blood from his mouth. Klimes and Liz were passive, each nodding occasionally.

I shifted my weight, trying to get comfortable with my hands behind my back. My right hand throbbed, and I was pretty sure I'd cut it on his teeth. I didn't care. He'd asked for it, and he knew what he was doing. I should have kept my cool, but I'd been doing that for two days now. Zanella had proven to be the antidote for my anger.

Liz and Klimes walked back to me.

"He's pissed, but he's not gonna charge you," she said. "He could, but Klimes talked him out of it."

"Don't make no sense, really," Klimes said with a shrug. "He said some things he shouldn't have, and you hit him, which you definitely shouldn't have. But he doesn't wanna have to explain to everyone how you dropped him."

"I'd be happy to tell people," I said.

"I'll bet," Klimes said, smiling. "Hey, Zanella's okay. Just wound a little tight and doesn't trust too many folks. Seeing too many dead people will do that to a guy. Specially a pretty girl like was in your place. But now we're dealing with this and you and he are gonna have to be around each other."

"No problem for me," I said.

Klimes chuckled and motioned for me to stand up. I did and he unlocked the cuffs.

"Make no mistake, though, Noah," he said, hooking the cuffs onto his belt loop. "Touch him again, and I'll shoot you." He aimed his index finger at me. "Got it?"

I examined my hand. Just scraped, no cuts. "Got it."

Klimes waddled away.

"You're lucky he's a good guy," Liz said. "Anybody else probably would've taken you inside and beat the shit out of you."

Klimes and Zanella walked around the other side of the house, Zanella throwing one last look over his shoulder at me.

"He nearly crushed me on the patio," I said.

"Big, strong guy."

"I'll say."

The people who had come outside for the altercation were filtering back into the house. My house. The one with the dead girl in it.

"I'm guessing I won't get to stay the night here," I said.

"Macho and smart," Liz said. "What a catch."

In the past, she would have been chewing me out for what I'd done. Not that I didn't deserve it. But now, she was cutting me some slack, probably knowing that the punch I'd thrown wasn't just for Zanella.

FIFTEEN

Liz and I walked up the boardwalk, away from the chaos that had enveloped my house. We were surrounded by bikers, skateboarders, and runners, but I felt more at home among them than I did with the cops and techs in my living room.

"First things first," she said. "You aren't a suspect. Obviously, I was with you thenight before last and was at your place until eight yesterday morning. They've confirmed you were on the plane and the visit to the prison. Zanella may be acting like an asshole, but they've cleared you."

I figured Zanella couldn't help acting the way he did. You are what you are.

A shirtless guy on rollerblades, bouncing to his iPod, sliced between us, the aroma of coconut oil swirling off him as he flew by.

A dull pounding was working my temples, a headache on the way. "Was she killed here?"

"Klimes said it doesn't look like it. Whoever did it brought her here already dead."

That explained the blood on the patio, but it didn't explain why. I thought of Darcy standing on the boardwalk, pressuring me to go see Simington. Tough and feisty.

"Any sign of a struggle?" I asked.

"They're checking."

I let out a long, slow sigh. A lot had gone on in the last twelve hours, and I didn't like any of it.

"Obviously, I won't be involved," Liz said. "Because of me and you. I called John. He'll keep an eye on it, stay in touch with Klimes and see where it goes."

Two middle-school-aged girls shrieked as two boys chased them up the sand, spraying them with water pistols.

"They brought her to my house for a reason," I said as the kids ran behind us.

Liz nodded. "I thought the same thing. Sending a message."

"A loud one. Darcy only came to see me about one thing. Means it has to be about Simington. Which is what I told Klimes and Zanella."

"So a dead Darcy is someone's way of telling you to stay out of it and away from him."

"Oops."

We did a U-turn and headed back toward the house. The dark clouds were still threatening but had failed to deliver a single drop of precipitation.

"How was San Quentin?" she asked. "Did you meet him?"

"Yeah. Simington's a swell guy." I waved a hand in the air, dismissing any of our conjecture that Darcy or Simington had been a fraud. "He's my father, Liz. No doubt."

She looked at me, her eyes heavy with concern. "I don't know what to say to that."

"I don't either."

"What was he like?"

"Looks like me. He wouldn't fight with me. Seemed to know how I was gonna feel about him. I was too numb to take in anything else, really." I paused. "And he had my name tattooed on his wrist."

She didn't say anything, waited for me to continue.

"He also gave me a name."

"A name?"

"Landon Keene," I said. "He said to start with that and see if I found anything."

"Name doesn't sound familiar," she said. "I'll run it and see if it pops."

"I honestly don't think he wants off death row," I said. "He didn't talk specifically about killing anyone, but he seemed at ease with what he'd done and where he is now."

She nodded. We kept walking.

"I met a cop who doesn't want him off, either," I said.

She raised an eyebrow in question. I told her about Kenney and what Miranda had told me.

She didn't seem surprised. "If he thinks Simington killed his nephew, it's a wonder he didn't just kill Simington himself."

"Yep."

"So that makes two then," Liz said.

"Two what?"

The breeze off the water ruffled through her hair. She pushed it away from her face.

"Two people who don't want Russell Simington leaving San Quentin," she said. "That cop and whoever killed Darcy Gill."

SIXTEEN

We'd arrived at my place just as Carter came barreling down the boardwalk on an old beach cruiser. He hit the brakes and skidded to a halt next to the wall.

He looked at the house, then me. "They find the meth lab?"

"Yeah. The jig is up."

Liz rolled her eyes. Carter smiled at her. They tolerated each other because of me. Being in the middle of them wasn't always easy, but I was learning to manage it a little better than in the past.

"I'll leave you two to . . . do whatever you do," Liz said. She put a hand on my shoulder. "I'll see you later."

"What the hell is all this?" Carter asked after she walked away.

"Remember the girl who came to see me?"

"Yeah."

"Dead. Inside."

He looked at me for a moment like he was trying to figure out if I was kidding. When he realized I wasn't, he said, "You didn't do it, did you?"

"Uh, no."

"Where were you?"

I hesitated. "San Francisco."

He frowned. "Why?"

"Went to meet the guy she said was my father."

"He lives up there?"

I took a deep breath. Telling Carter the whole truth would be a welcome relief; I could have used his help carrying this burden. I should've told him right away.

"He's a resident of San Quentin," I said.

"You serious?"

"Unfortunately. He's on death row."

He dropped his bike to the sidewalk and sat down on the wall next to me. "Oh, man."

I told him about my trip, and the end to any uncertainty that I was related to Russell Simington. I told him who Darcy was and why she'd come to see me. Something entered his expression halfway through my explanation, and I was pretty sure it was hurt. I was too chicken to address it.

"And now she's dead?" he asked when I'd finished.

"Yeah."

"Probably not a coincidence."

"No."

Out on the water, a couple of surfers were trying to make the small waves last a bit longer, bouncing and pivoting against the white water.

"How long have we been friends?" Carter asked.

"A long time."

"There's not much I've ever not told you," he said. "There've been some things you didn't want to know, but other than that, I think you know more about me than any other person on the planet."

I knew where he was heading, and I couldn't hide from it.

"Why didn't you tell me?" Carter asked.

"I don't know. I didn't know how to explain it, I guess."

"It doesn't matter to me, Noah. Shit like that won't ever matter to me."

The fact that he knew exactly why I hadn't told him made me feel worse.

"I know," I said. "It just caught me off guard, and I didn't know how to handle it."

He nodded slowly. "I could've gone with you or something. So you didn't have to do it alone."

"I needed to do it alone."

"Sure. Okay. But you still could've told me. Man, I knew something was off with you."

There weren't many people in my life who mattered enough to me to make me apologize for much. But Carter was one of them.

"I should've told you. I'm sorry. I just wasn't ready to tell anyone."

"You tell Liz?" he asked, glancing at me.

I didn't say anything, wishing I could get the right thing to come out of my mouth.

"Figured," he said, looking away.

The surfers who had been in the water were out of the ocean now, walking up the beach, the end of the day.

Carter stood, pulled his bike off the pavement, and swung a leg over the seat. "I wouldn't have kept something like that from you, Noah. For any reason. There's no one else I'd trust with that kind of thing." He paused, lifting one of his massive feetonto the pedals. "We've never judged each other, dude. You really think I was gonna start now? Because some guy shares your DNA?" He shook his head, then shrugged. "If you want my help, let me know."

He pedaled off.

SEVENTEEN

I hung out on the boardwalk for an hour, moping and worrying. I watched cops go in and out of my place. Occasionally, one of them would glance in my direction and give me a hard look, a silent warning that he knew what I'd done to Zanella.

I tried to look scared.

Klimes came out when they appeared to be shutting down for the night.

"Gonna have to keep you out tonight," he said, huffing and puffing. "Should be able to let you back in tomorrow, though."

"Can I get my hands on my laptop?"

"No can do. Still gotta dust it, and the tech boys will probably have a peek at the hard drive."

"You already cleared me."

"Not about you. Whoever offed the girl might've used the computer."

"Think they checked their email before shooting her?"

"Or did some shopping on eBay. Who knows?"

"Come on."

He grinned. "I'm a thorough son of a bitch, Noah."

I didn't like it, but Klimes was being a good cop.

He asked, "What do you need it for?"

"Just wanted to run a name."

He motioned to the alley. "Come on."

I followed him to a brown Crown Victoria. He opened the passenger door and waved me in. He went around to the driver's side.

He squeezed in behind the wheel and pointed to the laptop mounted on the dash. "That work for you?"

I shrugged. "I guess."

"What are you looking for?"

"Guy named Landon Keene. Can you look him up on Google?"

"Don't talk dirty to me," he said, smiling and navigating on the computer. He hit a few buttons, then shifted the screen in my direction. "There you go."

Two items popped up under the name. One was a high school football roster in Florida, listing Landon Keene as a sophomore lineman. The other had Landon Keene as a hairstylist in Alabama. I guessed that neither of those two was the Landon Keene who Russell Simington had told me about.

I swiveled the screen back to Klimes. "Thanks."

"Anything you wanna tell me about?"

"No," I said, not wanting to get into it. "Another thing I'm working on."

Klimes pursed his lips. "Alright. Ask you something?"

"Sure."

"This girl. Gill. Was she tough?"

I thought of her approaching me in the water and tailing me up the beach. "Seemed like it."

He thought about that, focusing on something over my shoulder. "What?" I asked.

"ME didn't see any sign of a struggle," he said.

"You think she got surprised?"

He rubbed a hand over his sweaty face. "That or she knew the cocksucker who shot her. Waits for her to turn around in conversation, then whammo. Maybe knocks her out, then does her with the gun."

"Somebody went to a lot of trouble, then," I said. "Killing her like that and taking the time to bring her to my house."

"Yep." Klimes shifted in the seat, the vinyl screaming beneath him. "You were the only reason she came down here?"

"Far as I know. That's what her paralegal said, too."

"Mind another question?"

I shook my head.

"You think you're gonna get your . . . this Simington off the row?"

I appreciated him not referring to him as my father, but it didn't change anything.

"No. I think Darcy thought she could, though."

"Doubtful," he said, shaking his head. "Just doesn't happen. So I'm glad you don't have any wild ideas." He looked at me. "And I hope that means you'll stay out of the way."

"She's in my house, Klimes."

"We'll get her out," he said, grinning. "I promise. But after that, I hope you'll let us do what we are paid so shittily to do."

I laughed. "I'll try."

"Good," he said, then waved me out of the car. "Zanella's gonna be here any second. Scoot."

I got out and shut the door.

The window slid down, and Klimes leaned over, his rotund face looking up at me. "You owe me."

"How do you figure?"

He held up three fingers. "I let you use the computer, I gave you the 'she didn't struggle' info, and I flattened you before Zanella could take your head off."

"Woulda been hard for him to take my head off while he was sitting on his ass."

He waggled a thick finger in front of me. "Whatever, son. You owe me. That Keene name rings a bell, I expect you to ring mine."

Klimes was sharp. He hadn't taken my bluff. I liked him. I didn't want to lie to him.

"Deal," I said, doing it anyway.

EIGHTEEN

The lights on the Coronado Bridge shone brightly in the early evening. The long gone sun had forgotten to take the heat of the day with it, and the wind blowing in my window as I crossed over to the island felt like an industrial-strength hair dryer.

Liz's house was perched on a nice little curve of street that fronted San Diego Bay. She was on the rooftop deck when I pulled up, and she waved me in the front door.

She was sitting in a beach chair, facing the lit-up buildings across the water. Her long, tan legs were stretched out in front of her, and she wore an old Chargers T-shirt and blue running shorts. She motioned with her beer to the small fridge on the corner of the deck.

"I splurged for you," she said.

I opened the fridge and found a bunch of Red Trolley bottles. I grabbed one and sat down in the empty chair next to her. "Thanks."

We sat in the dark for a while, drinking but not talking.

When it came to our relationship, Liz being a cop had a lot of drawbacks. But one of the things I appreciated most was that she understood silence was a necessary thing. It didn't mean anything was wrong or one of us was mad. It was just a way to decompress. Most people didn't understand that.

"Was it odd?" she asked as I grabbed us a couple of new beers.

I knew she was talking about Simington.

"Yes and no," I said. "In a lot of ways, it was like going to see someone I didn't know. Someone who wanted to hire me or something. Detached."

She nodded.

"But it was strange that he looked so much like me," I said, shaking my head. "Some people think Carolina and I look alike. But this was like looking down the road thirty years."

"Except you won't be in jail," she said.

I didn't say anything and took a drink.

"You know that, right?" she asked, glancing over at me.

I kept drinking.

"Don't confuse what he looks like with what he is, Noah. You're not him."

I'd said as much to Simington through the window, but that had been more of a defense mechanism than true belief. It was hard for me to separate the two.

"I've killed people," I said.

She pulled her legs in and sat up in the chair. "You think that makes you like him?"

"I think it means we share some of the same . . . abilities."

"No one has ever hired you to kill anyone. And if they tried, you wouldn't do it."

I shrugged, watching the lights bounce off the water.

"You were on the *right* side when those things happened," she said. "You never set out to kill them just for the sake of killing them. Or for money."

I wasn't so sure about that. It seemed trivial to distinguish between right and wrong when a life ended because of something I'd done. I wondered if there had been underlying reasons for the things I had participated in. Had I been more of a willing participant than I'd realized? Maybe sought out those situations to enact some sort of latent feelings I had? I'd killed when I thought my life was in danger, but now I was second guessing whether killing had really been necessary.

"Simington killed for a paycheck," Liz said. "I did some checking this afternoon. He was a brutally cold killer. Putting a bullet in the back of a head is a barbaric way to take a life. He's done it. You haven't. And he did it for no other reason than someone paid him to. He wasn't making a moral choice. He was doing his job."

I appreciated her belief in me, and while it didn't satisfy me, I didn't want to spend the evening dissecting my screwed-up psyche.

I reached over and held her hand. "Anything interesting in what you found on him?"

She hesitated. "You sure you wanna hear it?"

"No. But tell me anyway."

"What Darcy told you was basically true," she said. "The arrest reports made him as a hired gun. He drove these two guys out in the desert and took 'em out. The two vics had just crossed over a few days earlier."

"Was Simington a coyote? Bringing them over the border?"

She nodded. "At one time, it looks like. But a lot of that was guesswork because Simington wouldn't give up any names."

That didn't surprise me. The stoicism and calm I'd seen in him at the prison weren't fake. He seemed at ease with where he'd ended up, with no need to take anyone else with him.

"He was also in debt," Liz said.

"Surprise."

"Huge debt, though," she said. "Half a million."

"Wow."

"Appears he had a nasty gambling habit."

"Darcy mentioned he worked in some casinos."

"Yes, he did. And I did find one interesting consistency."

"What's that?"

"All three casinos that employed him are owned by a guy named Benjamin Moffitt. He owns Bareva out in Lakeside and a bunch of others."

"Any mention of a Landon Keene?" I asked.

"Nope."

I felt her fingers fold into mine, and we lapsed into silence again. The black water rippled in the distance, warped images of the skyline floating on top of the bay.

I didn't know what Liz was thinking about. But I knew where my thoughts were.

Benjamin Moffitt would be my starting point.

NINETEEN

I slept restlessly, images of Darcy Gill and Russell Simington clogging my mind for the better part of the night. I was out of bed early and did four hard miles next to the water, trying to clear my head and develop a plan. I knew I had to make one phone call to get the ball rolling, and it was the thing I was least looking forward to doing.

I was back at Liz's, sweating and tired, when I sat down on the front steps and dialed Carter on my cell.

He answered with a grunt.

"It's early, I know," I said.

"Then why the fuck are you making my phone ring?"

"Because we've got things to do."

"We?"

I was hoping he still thought of us as a *we* after the previous day's conversation. I knew I needed to explain to him a little more about why I'd kept him out of the loop, but I wasn't going to do it over the phone.

"Yeah. You interested?"

The line hummed for a moment. Then he said, "What are we doing?"

"Feel like gambling?"

"Vegas?"

"No. Lakeside."

"Blue hairs and penny slots?"

"You in or not?"

"Yeah."

"Want me to pick you up?"

He hesitated. "No. Where should I meet you?"

That stung me a bit. It was probably his way of staying pissed at me, and I couldn't blame him.

"Bareva Casino," I said.

"Noon alright?"

"Noon's fine."

"See you then."

I hung up and went inside to shower.

I checked on Liz after getting dressed. She was wrapped in the sheets like a mummy. I had a hard time sleeping in even when I did sleep well. She had a hard time getting up if she didn't have a reason. She had the day off, and there was no reason to disturb her. Plus, I knew she might try to dissuade me from going to the casino, and I didn't feel like being dissuaded. I left her a note telling her I'd call her later and headed out.

I stopped at a café on Orange to grab some breakfast. I got down an omelet and some juice before I realized I needed to make another phone call. I paid for my meal, walked outside, and dialed the Law Offices of Gill and Gill.

Miranda answered on the first ring, sounding more annoyed than she had yesterday.

"Miranda, it's Noah Braddock."

"Hold on. Let me get excited," she said.

I guessed from her tone that the police hadn't spoken to her yet. "I need to tell you something."

"Did you hear from Darcy?" she asked. "Because I haven't, and I'm starting to get pissed off about it. I've got people calling here looking for her, and I have no idea what to tell them. And I can't believe you just waltzed out of town without—"

"Miranda," I said. "Shut up and listen to me."

I could feel her making a face at the phone. "Fine. I'm listening."

I took a deep breath. "Darcy is dead."

"Funny, asshole. Shitty sense of humor."

"I'm not kidding, Miranda."

I watched several cars go by as I waited for her to say something.

"You're not kidding, are you?" she asked, her voice smaller, weaker.

"No. I wish I was. I found her body. She was in my house when I got back."

She cleared her throat. "Okay. I'm coming to San Diego."

"Well, you might want to wait until the police get in touch with you," I said. "They'll probably—"

"I'm coming," she said, and hung up.

TWENTY

Lakeside was a small community on the eastern outskirts of San Diego County. When I was growing up, it was one of those places that people made fun of as if it were three states away. But as the region grew, more and more folks moved out that way seeking affordable housing, and it was no longer a forgotten outpost. The Bareva Casino had only heightened the city's profile.

Reservation casinos were all the rage in southern California. The legality of gambling seemed grayer with the construction of each new cash cow in the nether regions of the county, and no one seemed to care. Throw up a huge monstrosity of a building with some neon lights and the chance to win money and people would come.

Bareva was no different. The casino was a castle-like structure lit up even in the afternoon. The massive parking lot was jammed with tour buses, motor coaches, and cars that had come from all over. It took me ten minutes to reach the entrance from where I left the Jeep.

Carter was waiting out front. He wore extra baggy cargo shorts, a neon-green Quiksilver T-shirt, and sandals. He was holding a Slurpee the size of a small trash can.

I motioned at the Slurpee. "Get me one?"

"Nope."

"Thanks."

He shrugged. "Figured we wouldn't look that tough if both of us had one."

"Oh."

"But if we don't have to look tough for whatever the fuck we are doing here, then I apologize." He stuck his tongue out and took a long lick on the straw. "And you can have mine." He held it out.

"I guess we'll have to look tough."

"Vindication." He nodded at the casino. "Are we here to try our luck?"

"Something like that," I said.

We walked inside. It might as well have been Las Vegas, with coins hitting trays, the relentless ringing of slot machines, bright lights, no clocks, and a noise level that made it hard to think. An occasional joyful scream as someone hit what they considered a jackpot. Old couples huddled at machines, slowly extracting quarters from a plastic bucket.

"Oh, I love the *Wheel of Fortune* one," Carter said, pointing at a giant machine with his Slurpee. "I wonder if they have *The Price is Right* one."

"I'll see if we can get you a roll of quarters."

We moved through the casino to a cage in the center that had an information sign. I asked where the administrative offices were, and we were pointed to a bank of elevators.

Riding up, Carter asked, "We applying for jobs?"

"Yeah, I thought you'd look great in one of those cocktail waitress outfits."

The elevator stopped, and the doors opened.

"Thank you for noticing," Carter said.

The admin floor felt like being miles away from the casino. Plush carpeting. Tasteful artwork on the walls. No incessant bell ringing. The elevator had transported us to another world.

An attractive woman with a bun of blond hair greeted us from behind an oak reception desk. "Gentlemen, how can I help you?"

Carter whispered, "Gentlemen?" and chuckled before he went back to sucking on his straw.

"We're looking for Ben Moffitt," I said.

"Do you have an appointment?"

"Do we need one?"

She smiled patiently. "Of course. Mr. Moffitt is a very busy man." She seemed to finally notice that we were dressed in shorts and T-shirts and one of us was enjoying a Slurpee. "Has there been a problem in the casino?"

"No, ma'am," I said. "We were just hoping to speak with Mr. Moffitt."

"Are you selling something?" she asked, squinting at us like that might help her figure us out.

"If you could tell him it's in regard to San Quentin, that would be great," I said, smiling.

She looked back and forth between us for a moment, then picked up the phone. She turned away from us as if she was looking at her computer, but I thought the move was more to keep us from hearing.

"Carolyn, I've got two young men out here asking to see Mr. Moffitt," she said, apology apparent in her voice. "Regarding San Quentin?"

She looked at me, smiled, and held up a finger to indicate it would be a second. I gave her a thumbs up. Carter moved the straw up and down in the lid so that it made a horrible groaning noise. She frowned in his direction. He gave her a thumbs up, too.

Her eyes moved away again. "Alright. Certainly. Thank you, Carolyn."

She hung up and swiveled back to us. "Gentlemen, I'm sorry. Mr. Moffitt's schedule is full today. If you'd like to leave a card, I can have his assistant get back with you to schedule a better time."

I pulled a card out of my pocket. "May I borrow a pen?"

She smiled, grateful that I wasn't going to fight her on it. She passed a pen to me.

I flipped the card over and wrote "Russell Simington" on the back. I slid the card and pen to her.

"I'd appreciate it if you'd take that to him right away," I said. "Tell him we'll be in the casino for a while. He can find us there."

She picked up the card. "I'd be happy to take this back, but I doubt he'll be able to see you today. But if he should ask, where in the casino might you be?"

I turned and headed for the elevator, Carter on my heels.

"We'll be the ones making a commotion," I said.

TWENTY-ONE

"Commotion?" Carter asked when the elevator let us out in the casino.

"Commotion," I said.

"You're not just teasing me, are you?"

"Nope. I needed something you were good at."

I thought he was going to start skipping, he looked so happy.

We went to the change cage, and I bought a hundred bucks in chips. I handed Carter half. Then we found a roulette table.

As we slid into the seats, I whispered to Carter, "Go crazy, dude."

He gave a tiny nod and set his Slurpee on the edge of the table.

A guy with dark hair and circles under his eyes greeted us. "Hello, gentlemen. Thank you for choosing Bareva. Place your bets, please."

"Sure thing, boss," I said. Then I looked at Carter and said louder than necessary, "I bet I'm gonna kick your ass here, bro."

"You and what person twice your size, bozo?" he said, matching my volume. He dropped a couple of chips on black. He glanced at the worker's nametag. "Fire her up, Bill, and make sure that fuckin' little pearl lands on black."

Bill laughed and turned to me. "Sir? Do you wish to bet?"

"I wanna be black," I said.

"So did Vanilla Ice," Carter said. "Let's go. Drop your money."

"You may also bet on black, sir," Bill said.

"No," I said, shaking my head. "I want to be the only one on black."

A perplexed expression settled on Bill's face.

I looked at Carter. "Next round, I'm black."

"Whatever, Vanilla." He pounded the edge of the table. "Come on. Let's go."

I dropped a couple of chips on red.

Bill spun the wheel. The tiny ball jumped like it was electrified.

"Come on, you little fucker!" Carter yelled, pounding the table again.

The ball bounced into the black slot and settled as the wheel came to a halt.

Carter stood and jumped up and down like a two-year-old in a crib. "Oh yeah, baby! Pay the big man!"

Bill laughed and slid some chips toward Carter. Carter reached for them, but I grabbed his wrist before he got there.

"That's my money," I said.

"The fuck it is, Vanilla," he said, appropriately appalled. "And you better let go of me before I make you eat this wheel."

"I called black."

"Too slow, bozo." He glanced at Bill, like can-you-believe-my-buddy. "Bill, that's my money, dude."

Bill now appeared as if he wished he'd called in sick. "Fellas, let's calm down."

People were creeping closer, unable to ignore our voices.

"My money," I said.

"My ass," Carter said.

I tackled him, and we fell to the floor.

"This is fun," Carter whispered as he rolled me over.

I wrapped my arms around his head. "Just you wait."

A flurry of people surrounded us and began pulling us apart. We both ended up in the arms of security guards. Lots of yelling and people telling us to calm down. For a moment, I wondered if our show was all for naught.

Finally, though, from the area near the elevators, three men in dark suits came toward us. Large, severe men.

I looked at Carter. "Here comes the real fun."

TWENTY-TWO

One of the suits took me by the arm. Not roughly, but more like he was escorting me around an art gallery.

He smiled politely. "Sir, if you'd like to come with us." It wasn't a question, but it lacked the threat I was expecting.

The two other suits gestured at Carter but didn't take his arm. A wise move.

We moved away from the scene of our lunacy and toward the elevators. My escort let go of my arm but was still smiling. "You succeeded in getting Mr. Moffitt's attention."

"Imagine," I said.

The elevator opened, and we all stepped in. I marveled that somewhere in the action Carter had managed to retain his Slurpee. He was sucking on the straw as if nothing had happened.

My escort stuck a key in a lock above the floor numbers and turned it. The doors closed, and we rose much higher than the fourth floor where we'd originally started. I guessed we went up about ten floors.

The doors opened, and the floor didn't look much different than the admin offices. The men escorted us into a conference room with a view of the hills and the afternoon sunshine. A crystal pitcher filled with water sat in the middle of a huge mahogany table, accompanied by six matching glasses.

My guy gestured at the plush leather chairs around the table. "Make yourselves comfortable, gentlemen."

We sat down, and they left.

Carter set his Slurpee on the table. "Now what?"

"Vanilla Ice?" I asked.

"You like that? I thought it was pretty good."

"I should've dumped the Slurpee on your head."

"Now that wouldn't have been good." He waved a hand around the room. "So?"

"So let's see who comes to visit us."

Twenty minutes and two glasses of water later, the door to the conference room opened. A guy a couple inches taller than me with a neck the size of a barrel led the way. His brown hair was buzzed short, and the skin on his face seemed stretched too tight, as if there weren't enough skin to cover his skull. Acne dotted his forehead. He scowled at us. He wore khaki pants and a black dress shirt with a butterfly collar that was open at his huge neck. Sweat stains darkened the shirt near his armpits. Lots of muscles in just about every place.

He was followed in by a man considerably shorter and less muscular. The second man was around five-ten with the build of a cross-country runner and shaggy black hair that hung to just above sleepy hazel eyes. He appeared to be trying to grow a goatee, but it didn't seem to want to come in. He wore white jeans and a bright purple polo shirt.

"Hi, fellas," he said. His voice was high-pitched and squeaky. "What are you here for?"

"Is either of you Benjamin Moffitt?" I asked.

"No. I'm Ross." He pointed at the gorilla, who had moved next to me. "That's Gus."

"We're here for Moffitt."

Gus's right hand shot out and drilled into the side of my head. My head snapped to the side and a rainbow of colors flashed in front of my eyes. Gus was strong.

"Easy, big guy," Ross said.

I shook my head, clearing the colors from my vision, and realized he was talking to Carter, who was halfway out of his seat. I held up a hand, and Carter sat back down.

Ross smiled in my direction. "Wanna try again?"

"We're here for Moffitt," I said. "Dickhead."

I felt Gus move again, but this time I was ready. I swept the pitcher off the table, swiveled in the chair, and smashed the pitcher into Gus's head. It disintegrated into a fine mist of water and glass when it hit his temple. His teeth snapped together like a bear trap, and he fell to the ground.

I looked at Ross, who was no longer smiling.

"Is Moffitt coming or do we need to go find him?" I asked.

Ross glanced at his partner. Gus was clutching the side of his head as blood percolated out of his mouth, his eyes shut tight in pain.

"I'll go get Mr. Moffitt," Ross said.

Carter stood. "We'll go with you."

"No need," Ross said, a little too quickly. "If you'll just wait here—"

"You can come back with who knows what," Carter said. He walked over and took Ross by the elbow. "Show us the way, buddy."

I stepped over Gus to follow them. The side of my head was still throbbing.

"Hang on," I said to Carter.

I turned around and drove my foot in Gus's solar plexus. The air whooshed out of him like a slashed tire, his eyes bulged, and his mouth opened into a silent, painful oval.

I pulled my foot off of him and faced an amused Carter and a worried Gus.

"Now let's go," I said.

TWENTY-THREE

Ross took us down a long hallway to a corner office. He knocked, timid, on the partially open door. A polite voice invited us in.

The room was huge and crescent-shaped, backed by a window that opened up to the expansive valley beyond the casino. Several leather chairs and a matching sofa sat around a glass coffee table in one corner. A magnificent mahogany desk was fronted with two more leather chairs. Our feet sunk into the plush carpeting.

Ben Moffitt leaned back in his chair behind the desk and smiled. "Hello, Ross. What's going on?"

Moffitt appeared to be in his early fifties. Dark hair that looked like it might have had some help in holding off the gray. Tan face. Bright, hazel eyes. A small pointed nose that fit perfectly over his small tight mouth. An expensive blue dress shirt opened at the neck. A gleaming watch on his left wrist.

Ross shifted his weight nervously. "Uh ... ah ... Mr. Moffitt ... these guys ... ah ... wanted to see you."

Moffitt nodded as if he'd been expecting us. "Fine. What can I do for you, gentlemen?"

"To start, you might want to call a doctor for Gus," I said, gesturing behind us. "His face is going to need some help."

Moffitt's eyes clouded over, confused. "Excuse me?"

"I don't like people hitting me in the head," I said. "Gus learned that the unfortunate way."

Moffitt frowned and moved his gaze to Ross. "Ross? What's he talking about?"

Ross shifted again, his feet kicking at the floor like he had to go to the bathroom. "Well, we didn't know ... uh ... I'm not ... they were in the casino and ..."

Moffitt held up a hand and shook his head. "Thank you, Ross. We'll speak more about this later."

Ross took the opportunity to pivot and slink out of the room.

Moffitt stood and held out his hand. "I'm Ben Moffitt. I apologize for any trouble you encountered."

I shook his hand and was taken aback. I'd expected to walk into an unfriendly room. Moffitt was treating us like long lost friends.

"I'm Noah," I said.

He held out his hand to Carter. "I'm Ben Moffitt."

Carter hesitated, then shook his hand. "Carter."

Moffitt gave a sharp nod and gestured for us to sit down in the chairs that faced his desk. We did, and he eased down into his own chair.

"Again, I apologize for any trouble Gus and Ross may have given you," he said, forcing a reluctant smile onto his face. "Sometimes they get a little excited and don't make the appropriate decisions."

I nodded. "It's fine."

"I'll make sure we make it up to you," Moffitt said.

"No need," I said. "Really."

"Well, we'll see," Moffitt said. He smiled again, showing some coffee-stained teeth. "Now, how can I help you?"

"Hold on a sec," Carter said. "I'm confused."

"How so?"

"We came up here half an hour ago, and it was all your receptionist could do to shoo us back into the elevator," he said. "Then we get your attention in the casino, Tweedle-Dum and Tweedle-Dumbass try to put the squeeze on us, and now we're sitting here and you seem happy to see us?"

Moffitt looked amused. "First off, the receptionist is instructed to turn away anyone looking to see me. If I made myself available to every person who lost twenty bucks in my casino, I'd never get anything done." He smiled. "I don't know what you're referring to in the casino. Gus is one of my heads of security. He's instructed to handle situations." His smile dimmed. "What he's not instructed to do is harass our patrons, regardless of what has occurred." He leaned forward. "My willingness to speak to you is my way of apologizing for the inappropriate treatment you may have experienced."

Moffitt was smooth, polished. Just like the room. I thought it was interesting that he hadn't asked what occurred downstairs. I wasn't sure whether to believe him or not. But I had a difficult time thinking he didn't know about every little thing that was happening in his casino.

"I'm an investigator," I said.

"Not from the gaming commission, I hope," Moffitt said, chuckling.

"No. I'm working for a man named Russell Simington."

I watched for a reaction but saw nothing.

"Should I know that name?" Moffitt asked.

"I believe he worked for you."

"Mr. Braddock, I've got over two thousand employees working in my casinos," he said. "I wish I knew them all by name, but I don't."

"He's in jail now."

Moffitt leaned back in his chair.

"On death row," I said.

Moffitt still showed nothing.

Carter reached over to the edge of the desk and picked up a medium-sized crystal paper weight. It was shaped like a large egg, and it looked expensive. He turned it over in his hands, examining it.

Moffitt started to say something, then stopped.

"I've been told he worked for you," I said.

"I can certainly check to see if that's accurate," Moffitt said, looking from me to Carter and back to me.

"Name doesn't sound the least bit familiar?"

Moffitt shook his head. "No, I'm sorry. Like I said, two thousand is a big number. But I'll be happy to have Human Resources check the name. I can have someone get you the information by tomorrow morning." He paused. "Why is he facing execution?"

Carter tossed the paperweight up in the air and let it fall back into his hands. He threw it again, a little higher this time, and had to reach behind himself to make the catch.

Moffitt cleared his throat but said nothing.

"He killed two men," I said.

Moffitt gave a small wince. "Wow."

"Yeah."

Carter set the crystal egg back on the desk. Moffitt hesitated for a moment, then reached over and repositioned the egg a fraction of an inch.

He leaned back in his chair, looking more relaxed now. "Can I ask why you'd choose to work for someone like that?"

A loaded question if I'd ever heard one. But I wasn't about to explain the complicated situation involving my father.

"I'm just checking into some things," I said. "How about Landon Keene?"

Moffitt raised an eyebrow. "Another employee?"

"Yes."

He thought about it, then shook his head. "Don't recognize that name, either. But I'll be happy to have my people research that as well."

If he knew anything, he wasn't going to give it up. And his act was so good, I wasn't sure if it was an act.

"May I ask how my name came up?" he asked.

"Basic background checks," I lied. "Employment history and things like that. Figured I'd start at the top. I'm just looking to get a few things corroborated."

"Of course," he said, seeming satisfied. "Well, as I said, it's impossible for me to know the names of everyone who works here. But we keep diligent records. If either of them were employed here, we'll be able to tell you exactly when they were here and what they did." He opened a drawer, pulled out a card, and slid it across the desk. *Susan Hayward, Vice President of Human Resources* was printed on it, along with a phone number. "I'll let Susan know you'll be calling tomorrow morning. She'll be able to give you your answers."

It seemed like an invitation to leave. Carter and I stood. Moffitt came around the desk and walked us to the door.

He held out a hand. "I'm sorry again for the incident, Mr. Braddock."

I shook his hand and smiled. "No problem."

He and Carter shook hands.

"Come back and visit us anytime," Moffitt said.

"Right," Carter said.

We walked down the hallway to the elevator. No sign of Gus or Ross.

The bell above the elevator dinged, and we stepped in.

"Guy's a goddamn psychic," Carter said.

"I'll say," I said, pushing the button for the lobby and watching the doors close. "Dude knew my last name even though I never gave it to him."

TWENTY-FOUR

"He was completely full of shit, right?" Carter asked as we stepped off the elevator and back into the casino.

"Pretty close to completely."

"He really expected us to believe those guys grabbed us down here and he didn't know?"

"Two people fighting in the casino," I said, looking around at the blinking lights and crowd of people. "They didn't know who we were, they would've just thrown us out the door and told us to stay out."

"Exactly."

Maybe Moffitt had acted like he didn't know the names I'd thrown at him, but he knew who we were and he had Gus and Ross bring us up to scare us off. We'd touched on something.

"What the hell's wrong with that guy?" Carter said, nodding in the direction of the closest bank of slot machines.

A well-built guy about six feet tall, in black jeans and a horrible Hawaiian shirt, was in the face of a slightly smaller man. He had blond hair and a matching goatee, and he was stabbing his finger repeatedly in the man's chest. The smaller man didn't look scared, but he didn't look all that happy, either. Embarrassed, maybe.

I couldn't make out the conversation over the din of the room. The goateed guy crowded him a little more, bullying like a good bully. The smaller man finally took a step back, turned, and walked away.

The bully watched him go, then moved in our direction.

"The fuck are you looking at?" he growled, taking a couple more steps.

"The ugliest shirt I've ever seen," Carter said, leaning forward, staring in amazement. "Pelicans, hula girls, and ukuleles? Was the shirt covered in dog shit sold out?"

The guy's face reddened, and he glanced down at his outfit.

"You take that guy's lunch money?" I asked.

He jerked his head up and took a few more steps so that he was just a couple of feet from us now. "Excuse me?"

"You're excused," I said.

He looked back and forth between me and Carter. We were both bigger than he was, but that didn't seem to intimidate him.

"Why don't you mind your own fucking business?" he said.

"Why don't you show us how?" Carter said, grinning.

They stared at each other.

"Fuck off," the guy finally said.

"That's what I thought," Carter said, still grinning.

The guy moved his gaze to me. His eyes were slate gray and there was a fading, jagged scar under the left one. His flat nose was a little crooked. I had a feeling he was used to mixing it up. Maybe even liked it.

I had put him in his thirties when I'd first seen him, but up close, I realized he was somewhere north of that. Years of starting fights might give you a nice physique, but you couldn't hide the wear and tear on your face.

His eyes flickered, and I thought he was going to start with me.

But then the right side of his mouth curled into something between a smile and a grimace, and he chuckled. He spun on his heel and walked back into the circus of bells, slots, and noise. He went all the way through the gaming floor, turned left down a hallway, and disappeared, never looking back.

"This place is awesome," Carter said.

"Let's get out of here."

We walked outside, the midday sunlight startling after the muted lighting inside.

I shaded my eyes with my hand. "Thanks for driving out here."

"Nothing I like better than a drive out to the boonies with nothing to show for it," Carter said. "No problem. What's next?"

"I'm not sure," I said.

And that was the truth. I didn't know where to head next. We could go back up and strong-arm Moffitt, but I wasn't sure that was a wise move. He knew something, but until I knew what it was, I couldn't just walk in and kick his ass.

"Alright," Carter said. "Call me when you do."

"Hey," I said, as he walked off. "Are we cool?"

He paused, thinking about it for a moment, his features silhouetted against the bright daylight. We had morphed back into our usual routine while we were in the casino, but it still felt like there was something hanging in the air between us.

"We're getting there," he said.

He headed off for his car, and I figured that was as fair of a response as I could expect.

I walked across the parking lot and got into the Jeep. Then I started it up and zig-zagged through the aisles, heading for the exit. As I passed the front entrance, I glanced at the giant glass doors and up higher at the top floor where Moffitt's office was housed.

A figure in a window directly above the entrance caught my attention.

I hit the brakes, checked the mirror to make sure no one was behind me, then looked back up to the window.

It was empty.

I let the Jeep idle for a moment and watched the window to see if anyone returned.

It stayed empty.

Finally, I stepped on the gas and headed out of the lot, wondering what that goateed bully was doing staring down at me.

TWENTY-FIVE

The next day, I decided on a different tact. I was frustrated at making little headway and learning virtually nothing about Simington. I knew there was one person who would be able to provide some information, and I had avoided her long enough.

I needed to talk with my mother.

Carolina Braddock and I had reached something resembling a truce for the previous few months. We talked a couple of times a month, had dinner or lunch at least once. I tried to be pleasant, and she tried not to be drunk. We hadn't erased the discord of the past, but we seemed to be moving forward rather than stalled in the yesteryears.

As I pulled up in front of her house, the place I grew up in and sprinted from the day I was able, I reminded myself that this wasn't a social call.

This would be business.

The house looked the same as it always did. Not great, not awful. Just indifferent. Patches of brown grass. Cracks in the driveway. Faded paint. Dusty windows. A garage door that never hit the ground squarely.

I stuck my finger on the doorbell and wondered if it would ever change.

Carolina appeared behind the screen door.

"Noah," she said. "This is unexpected."

My antenna went up. "Pleasant surprise" would have meant she was happy to see me. "Unexpected" said to me that she was partially into a bottle. But this wasn't a prearranged meeting, so our truce rules weren't in play.

"Sorry," I said. "I didn't think to call. Can I come in for a minute?"

"Of course," she said, pushing the screen open and letting me through.

The living room hadn't changed a second since I'd been a kid. Same brown corduroy couch and loveseat. An old, cheap coffee table that sported faint crayon marks. Shag carpet that had moved from beige to dirty beige. An old console television against the wall. An attempt to freshen things up with the odor of Lysol.

My childhood tried a full-scale rush into my head, but I slammed the door.

"Sit, sit," she said, moving the newspaper off the sofa.

She wore a faded blue sweatshirt and jeans. Her brownish-blond hair was pulled away from her face and back into a rubber band. She still looked ten years younger than her age.

"I wasn't expecting company," she said, straightening the magazines on the table. "So sorry it's a mess."

"It's fine. I didn't mean to barge in."

"You're never barging. Would you like something to drink?"

In this house, that question always felt like a powder keg.

"No, I'm good," I said.

Carolina walked over to the Formica dining room table and picked up a half-empty plastic tumbler. Ice and what looked like lemonade. A slight misstep as she turned back around forced her to catch herself and regain her balance.

Not just lemonade.

She smiled and came back to the sofa, tumbler in hand. "So. How are you?"

"I'm okay," I said, wondering if the lemonade contained vodka or gin. She loved them both. "You?"

She took a sip of the drink and smiled again. "Good. Really."

Maybe we had agreed to a truce, but there was nothing we could do about the awkwardness of it all.

"I need to ask you about something," I said.

She held the cup in both hands, her delicate fingers around it like a vice. "Alright."

"Actually about someone."

Her eyes were clear, interested in what I was saying. "Okay."

"Tell me about Russell Simington."

Her fingers flinched on the big tumbler and anxiety filled the edges around her light blue eyes. She held the tumbler up to her mouth and took a long drink. She brought it down and set it on the table. She readjusted herself on the sofa cushion, her back ramrod straight.

"I haven't heard that name in quite some time," she said.

"I'd never heard it until a couple of days ago."

She folded her hands together, then unfolded them, like she didn't know what to do with them. I couldn't blame her. I had just showed up and thrown his name out there. She had probably been wondering what she was going to have to drink with dinner.

"Is this about my never telling you about him?" she asked. "Because you never asked."

"No, it's not about that," I said. "You're right. I never asked because I didn't care. I'm not sure that I do now. But a lawyer came to see me."

Alarm flashed through her eyes. "A lawyer? Why? What does he want from you? He never wanted anything to do with us before."

"He's in prison," I said. "On death row."

She processed that, her mouth a tight line. "Unfortunately, I can't say I'm surprised. Russell always seemed headed for something like that."

I moved back into the sofa, ready to let her talk.

She cleared her throat and stared at the tumbler, but didn't reach for it.

"We met in a bar," she said, a sad smile forming on her face. "I'm sure that's no great revelation for you. It was out in El Cajon somewhere. I was with friends, and he was shooting pool. We struck up a conversation. He was polite, funny, charming."

I'd been in a few bars in El Cajon. I'd never seen anyone with those three qualities patronizing them. More like rough, violent, drunk. But I let her go on.

"We dated for a few months," she said. "He was into some bad things. He didn't work, but he always had money. There were always hideous-looking people coming to his apartment at all hours of the night."

"Did you know what those bad things were?" I asked.

"No," she said, glancing at me. "I didn't ask. He had a temper, and it always felt like one of those questions that wasn't possible. And I probably didn't want to know. I was starting to fall in love with him."

The image of Carolina and Russell together didn't fit in my head. But maybe that was because I couldn't picture him in any way other than behind that glass, in that jumpsuit.

"I got pregnant," she said, running a hand over her hair. "At first, he seemed to care. He was attentive, we talked a little about the future. I was excited. I wanted a baby. Maybe needed one, to give me direction. I don't know. Then he came over to my apartment one night. With a gun." She paused, clearly remembering the moment. "I asked him what it was for and he told me that he needed it, that he couldn't take any chances. Very vague, but adamant. I told him that if we were going to have a child, he couldn't keep going like that, doing whatever he was doing. I didn't want that around my child. We fought, and he left." She chewed her bottom lip, hesitating. "I wasn't always a mess, Noah. I'm not sure how or why it turned, but back then? I thought I could be a good parent."

She reached for the tumbler, stared into it for a moment, then took a drink, closing her eyes.

She placed it on the table again and swung her eyes to me, as sad as I had ever seen them in my lifetime.

"I never saw him again," she said.

TWENTY-SIX

We sat there in silence for a few minutes, and I felt like a teenager again. The prolonged periods of quiet in that house were some of my loudest memories. Sunday afternoons especially. Carolina emerging from a long, absorbed night of drinking, where all she could do was sit and hope for the hangover to dissolve, while I sat on the sofa watching football on mute, wanting desperately for her to be different.

But it was always quiet.

"What did he do?" Carolina asked.

"Killed two men."

If that surprised her, she didn't show it.

"Are you trying to get him out of prison?"

"I'm not clear on what I'm trying to do yet," I said. "His lawyer came to me, told me about him, wanted my help. But Simington didn't tell me much."

Carolina sat up straight again, as if she'd been poked with a live wire. "You've seen him?"

"Yeah."

She started to say something, then stopped. She glanced at the drink on the table. I wanted to kick it, send it flying.

But she didn't reach for it.

"That had to have been difficult," she finally said.

"Wasn't the most enjoyable thing I've ever done."

"Then you know how much you . . ." she said, her voice trailing off.

"Look like him?" I said, agitated at hearing the comparison again. "Yeah. I get it."

She picked up the tumbler and held it in her lap like a child would hold her favorite stuffed animal or blanket. For comfort.

"I am sorry that he is your father," she said.

There was nothing for me to say to that, so I didn't respond.

"I've never regretted not looking for him or trying to drag him into your life," she said, spinning the cup slowly in her hands. "I knew the question was always there for you, even though you never asked. But I knew who Russell was. I may have brought other problems into your life, but I always felt like that was different from what he would have brought."

I wanted to feel reluctant about that, but she was right. Being raised by an alcoholic was the preferred choice to being raised by a criminal. Still, I knew I would always have the feeling that I was cheated somewhere along the line.

"You never saw him again," I said. "Did you ever talk to him?"

She stared into the tumbler. "Twice."

"When?"

"Once when you were about five," she said. "He called me. I don't know how he found the number. Said he wanted to start sending me money to help." The bittersweet effect of the call was etched on her face. "I said okay. And he lived up to it, I guess. Sent cash in an envelope every so often. I put it all in an account that I used for you."

I tried to remember bringing in the mail as a kid, wondering if I'd held one of those envelopes in my hand.

"And the other time?"

She hesitated, took a tiny sip from the drink, and slid the cup onto the table. She ran the heels of her hands down the length of her thighs, like she was trying to push something away that wasn't there.

"It was a year after you'd moved out," she said. "He called again. He wanted to know where you lived."

That explained where he got the information about me he'd given Darcy. It didn't make me happy, though.

"I tried to blow him off," Carolina said. "But he was persistent. And when he brought up the fact that he'd sent some money over the years, I gave in and told him."

"How much of that money did I see and how much did the liquor stores see?" The bitterness in my voice surprised me.

She stared at me for a moment, then stood and walked carefully into the dining room, her back to me. She placed her hands on the edge of the table, then turned back to me.

Her face was flushed, her eyes lit with rage.

"You have no idea what it is like to be left alone and pregnant," she said, her voice bordering on yelling. "No idea. I am nowhere near perfect, and I have never, ever claimed to be. But I chose *you*. Not him. I chose you." The veins in her neck were pulsing, and she was yelling now. "So you can sit there, comfortable in your life and who you are now, and try to belittle me all you want. But I won't let you rip away the fact that I am proud of that choice!"

I felt the heat rush up the back of my neck and into my face. I looked down at the carpeting.

After a moment, she cleared her throat and sat back down in the chair.

"You saw it all, Noah," she said, an angry edge to her voice. "Every penny. I may have screwed up a lot of other things around here, but that money was meant for you and I did nothing other than feed and clothe you with it. It bought you a surfboard on your sixteenth birthday, and it was the spending money that magically filled your pockets in high school."

The silence gobbled up the room for a few minutes before I was able to look at her.

On cue, she picked up the tumbler from the table and held it to her lips, her eyes piercing me as she drank. Some sort of defiant message meant to make me feel like a jerk.

It worked.

"Did you ever get any sense of what he was into?" I asked, choosing to coward out of an apology.

She took a deep breath and shook her head. "Not really. Like I said, I don't think he would have answered even if I had asked. He would disappear for days at a time, and as time went on, before he left, it became more difficult for me to find the courage to ask what he was doing."

"When he disappeared. Do you know where he went?"

"I know he went to Las Vegas a lot," she said, her eyes flickering. "He would bring back matchbooks from the hotels. Other than that, I don't know."

It struck me as more than coincidental that casinos kept coming up when I asked about Russell Simington.

I stood up. "I gotta go."

She walked me to the door, and we stood there awkwardly for a few moments.

"Will they really kill him?" she asked, staring past me out the screen door.

"Seems like it. From what little I know, there's no reason not to."

She nodded slowly, her eyes focused on something I couldn't see. Maybe the past.

"I'm sorry," she said. "That you had to learn about him like this. And that he turned out like he has."

I opened the screen door. "It's not your fault. He is who he is." I paused. "You were right to keep him away from us."

Her eyes moved from whatever she had been looking at to me. It was probably the first time I had ever complimented anything resembling her parenting skills. She looked as surprised to hear it as I felt for having said it.

"Be careful, Noah," she said, reaching out and touching my elbow. "You've managed this long without him. There was very little good in his life, and I can't imagine anything has changed." Her eyes were sharp, clear. "Don't let him hurt you now."

TWENTY-SEVEN

I stopped for a sandwich at a deli on Grand before venturing back to Mission Beach to see if I could get back into my house.

As I navigated the streets, I listened to Jason Mraz croon on the radio and thought about what Carolina had told me. Most of what she'd said hadn't been a surprise. Meeting in a bar, lives that didn't mesh, those were things that I expected.

Sending money every month was a shock, though. To learn that someone who I had never considered part of my life had indeed been a very large part was unsettling. On one hand, it was a kind gesture that probably helped us out more than I'd ever know. But on the other hand, the one that hit me like a fist, why had Simington chosen to participate from a distance if he truly had an interest in my life?

I wrestled with that as I drove down Mission Boulevard. I turned onto Jamaica and found the alley clogged with midday traffic. I had to park two blocks away and walk up the boardwalk. The crime scene tape was gone from the perimeter, but a familiar face greeted me from my patio.

Miranda was sitting in one of the lounge chairs, a backpack next to her. She was wearing the same outfit of death she had on when I met her, black on black, with gigantic black sunglasses shading her face.

She saw me and sat up. "Where have you been?"

I stepped over the wall onto the patio. "What?"

"I told you I was coming."

"I know."

She sighed, disgusted by my inability to comprehend.

"You didn't say when, and I wouldn't have waited around any-way." I sat at the table next to the chairs and unwrapped the sandwich. "You want half? It's roast beef and turkey."

She looked at it and made a face. "I don't eat meat."

"Surprise, surprise."

She twisted around, looking inside my place. "They found Darcy here?"

"Yeah," I said. In between bites, I told her what I knew.

Miranda adjusted the glasses on her stark white face. "She was really good to me."

I nodded slowly and worked on the sandwich. The sun was spar-kling across the ocean, the white water looking like snow atop clear blue waves. Most days, I could have sat there and watched it for hours, letting everything else wait and fall away.

"You're sure she wasn't meeting with anyone else here?" I asked.

"Not that I know of," she said, finally pulling her eyes off the glass door. She glanced up at the sun like it had crapped on her shoulder. "Jesus, it's hot."

I finished the sandwich and balled up the foil it had come in. "Wanna go inside?"

She glanced at the sliding door again, then looked at me. "No."

I couldn't blame her. I wasn't looking forward to going inside either. A lot of things had happened in my place in the years I'd lived there, but this was the first time it had housed a dead person.

"I brought the files," Miranda said. "Everything I could find."

"Great," I said. "Darcy have any family?"

"I don't think she was conceived immaculately," she said. "But I never met them."

Good to see Miranda hadn't lost her edge.

"So what are you going to do?" she asked.

"I don't know yet."

"Yet? What are you waiting for?"

I knew Miranda was probably having a tough time of it. Her friend and boss had been killed. She'd flown down at a moment's notice with no plan.

But I didn't need her shit.

"Miranda, let's get something straight," I said, staring at her.

She returned the stare, the giant oversized sunglasses making her look like a bumblebee.

"If you think you're gonna hang out here and run the show, you can forget it. Darcy brought a bunch of crap into my life that I'm still trying to get in order, and I'm not sure how long that's gonna take. And I'm sorry about what's happened to her, and if I can help the cops figure it out, I will." I reached over and pulled the sunglasses down her nose so I could see her eyes. "But if you give me a single second of shit over any of this, I'll stuff you in the coffin you arrived in and float you out to Hawaii." I pushed the glasses back into place.

I turned away from her and settled into my chair, closing my eyes and letting the sun warm my face.

After a moment, Miranda said, "Fine."

I opened an eye and saw her lay back in the lounge chair. "Yep. It is."

"But Darcy was right about one thing," she said.

I shut the eye again and went back to feeling the sun. "What was that?"

"You really are kind of a dick."

TWENTY-EIGHT

"What do you know about the two men Simington killed?" I asked.

"Not much," Miranda answered, tilting her head in my direction. "They were Mexican nationals, probably with fake working papers."

The papers weren't hard to get and neither was work. If you were willing to take money under the table and endure the risk, anyone coming over the border illegally could find employment.

"Were their families ever interviewed?" I asked.

Miranda thought about that, then shook her head. "No, I don't think so. I'm not sure that they were in the States. Most of the information about them came from your father in his confession."

That didn't surprise me. Two illegal aliens involved in criminal activity. No one on this side of the border would have cared enough to track down their families. And once they got the guy they wanted—Simington—it was case closed.

I was pondering that when Detectives Klimes and Zanella came strolling up the boardwalk.

Klimes held up a fat hand in greeting. Even his sweat had sweat on it. "Afternoon, Noah."

Zanella glared at me and didn't say anything.

I smiled at Zanella, then looked at Klimes. "Hey."

Klimes nodded at Miranda. "Hello, miss."

She sat up in the lounge chair and pulled the glasses off her face, squinting at him but saying nothing.

"You are?" Klimes asked, with a smile.

"Hotter than hell," she said, frowning at him. "Who are you?"

"Detective Klimes with the San Diego PD," he said, still smiling. He motioned at his partner. "This is Detective Zanella."

Zanella was still glaring at me.

"This is Miranda," I said. "She worked for Darcy Gill."

Klimes raised an eyebrow. "Really? Tremendous. Saves me some time. Would you mind taking a walk with Detective Zanella so he might ask you a few questions?"

She cocked her head at Zanella. "What happened to your mouth? It looks like someone punched you."

The muscles around Zanella's jaw quivered, the various shades of purple at the corner of his mouth flushing. I thought I could make out the imprints of my knuckles in the bruising, but I wasn't sure.

"Miranda," Klimes said, offering her a big hand to pull herself up. "Would you mind?"

She looked at me, and I nodded.

Klimes helped her up, and she stepped over the wall next to Zanella.

She leaned in closer to him. "Are your teeth loose?"

Zanella glanced at me and then led her down the boardwalk.

Klimes fell into the chair Miranda had been sitting in. "Gonna take Zanella awhile to get over that punch."

"Gonna take me awhile to get over his being such an asshole."

"I love a good catfight," Klimes said, letting out a chuckle. "We got a description of a guy in the area around here early this morning."

"Someone saw something?"

"Two people gave us the same rough description," he said, wiping the sweat off his forehead with his hand. "A man, on the boardwalk about an hour before we got your call."

"Was he with Darcy?"

"No. Alone. But both wits said this guy looked out of place. Moving too fast, head down, unfriendly. Male, about six feet, not sure on the age," he said. "Not much else to distinguish him."

"If we sit here for five more minutes, we're gonna see at least five guys go by that fit that, Klimes."

He shaded his eyes from the sun. "I know. We're gonna do some door to door and see if we can turn anything else up." He shifted in the chair, the seat groaning beneath his bulk. "You run across anything new?"

"Not really."

"No, or not really?"

"No."

"That name you tried to slip by me the other day? I ran it through our computers."

"Landon Keene?"

"That's the one. Couple of things. Assaults, weapons. Done some time."

"Anything else?"

"Nope. So where did that name come from?"

I thought of my father tossing it out there, like bait. I had bitten, and yet it had gotten me nowhere.

"I don't know who he is," I said. "But if I find out, I'll tell you, Klimes. I promise."

He studied me for a moment, his eyes hard. "Not what I asked." He smiled, letting me know he knew I was avoiding the question. "But I'll settle for that for now."

"You know anything about a Benjamin Moffitt?" I asked.

"The casino guy?" Klimes said. He rolled his massive shoulders and shrugged. "Like all those types, you hear rumors."

"What kind of rumors?"

"Gaming industry never brings in the cleanest folks, you know? There's always some doubt as to the legitimacy of those running them. Nature of the business."

"Anything specific on Moffitt?"

"Nothing specific enough to get a hard-on over," Klimes said. "Some whispers about money laundering, maybe some payoffs to the gaming regulators. Nothing that would make him any different from his peers." His eyes sharpened. "Why?"

"Simington was employed as a security guard. At casinos owned by Moffitt."

Klimes rubbed a perspiring hand across his chin. "Well, wouldn't be the first time a piece of crap worked in that job. No guarantee that Moffitt even knew him, though. Not like he's gonna mix with the help."

"Sure."

"Coulda been a guy like Simington, with all those debts, was working it off." Klimes shrugged again. "I don't know. I'll ask around."

Miranda and Zanella appeared at the wall.

"All set?" Klimes asked.

Zanella glared at me. "Yeah. All set."

I smiled at him. His eyes iced over.

"You'll be in town for a while, young lady?" Klimes asked.

Miranda shrugged. "I don't know. I just got here before Mr. Charm dragged me away and asked me a bunch of questions that he must've learned from *Miami Vice*."

I laughed out loud. Zanella's eyes narrowed into tiny razor blades.

"Let us know if you leave," Klimes said. He put a hand on Zanella's shoulder. "Let's ride, buddy."

They started walking down the boardwalk.

Zanella was so predictable. I knew he'd turn around and throw a hard look my way.

Eventually, he did.

And before I could do it, Miranda blew him a kiss and showed him her middle finger.

TWENTY-NINE

I told Miranda she could stay with me.

"Don't get your hopes up," she said upon accepting the invitation. "I'll be sleeping nowhere but the couch."

"I'll try to keep my raging desire in check," I said, shaking my head.

I gave her a key and said I'd be back later.

"I have to go in there by myself?" she asked, glancing toward the patio door.

"No," I said, heading down the boardwalk. "You can sit right there and wait however many hours it takes me to come back. And then I'd be happy to escort you in."

I was pretty sure she was flipping me off behind my back, but I didn't turn around to confirm.

I was exhausted and needed some quiet, some familiarity. I called Liz and left her a message, telling her I was coming over.

By the time I'd navigated the traffic out of Mission Beach, down I-5, and over the bridge to Coronado, she was waiting for me on the front steps of her house.

She wore a Padres T-shirt with the sleeves cut off, khaki capris, and white flip-flops.

She stood. "You look tired."

"I am."

"Well, too bad."

"What?"

She pointed to her car, a gray Volkswagen Jetta. Two surfboards were strapped on top: the long, soft board I had bought for her to learn on and the six-three Rusty I'd started leaving in her garage.

"I thought we could go out for a while," she said, sounding like a kid whose parent had just arrived home.

We'd taken a trip to Santa Barbara a few months back, and I'd gotten her on a board. Now she was hooked and getting good. I liked that she liked it. I didn't know if it was coincidence that our relationship had finally come together when she took up surfing, but I liked the parallel anyway.

"Okay," I said. "Lemme go in and change."

"Can I watch?" she asked, as I passed her and headed into the house.

"Might not get to the water."

"You wish."

I changed—alone—and ten minutes later we were standing on the sand at a strip of beach just north of the Hotel Del. So late in the day, with the sun getting ready to wave goodbye, we had the place to ourselves.

"You're going to be amazed when you see me ride," she said with a grin, pulling off the T-shirt and capris to expose white bikini bottoms and a matching white rash guard.

If the beach had been full, it would have come to a standstill.

I refocused. "You've been practicing on your own?"

"You'll see."

It didn't surprise me. She'd nearly had a fit the first hour she'd been in the water with a board. She was strong and athletic, but learning to get your feet in the right spot and your weight balanced was tough for everyone. Getting up and falling over right away had not thrilled her. She'd eventually gotten the hang of it, but she still had that I'm-new-at-this pose on the board and it irked her. She wanted to look like she belonged, and she'd probably been doing pop-ups in her living room every day to get it right.

We waded in and got out to just in front of the break line so she'd have some strong white water to use.

"Have at it," I said.

She turned herself around, slid onto the board, checked behind her, and started paddling just before a big surge of water pushed into her. It propelled her forward and two seconds later she was up. Knees bent, relaxed, actually trying to maneuver the board with her back foot.

She had been practicing.

She looked back at me to make sure I'd seen her, then jumped off and paddled back out to me.

"I'm impressed," I said.

She pushed the wet hair off her face. "As you should be."

"You ready to paddle into something real?"

"Bring it on."

We paddled out a little further, just beyond the break line. The sets were small but rolling pretty consistently, no more than three feet high.

"Watch when I start paddling," I said, spinning myself around. "And then when I pop."

The wave came in behind, rising sharply out of the ocean. I paddled hard for a couple of seconds, letting it pick me up. I could feel the speed of the wave and knew I had it. At the top, I moved to my feet and guided the board down the small face and along the bottom of the wave. I snapped the board back up into the lip, pointing it almost straight up at the sky, spraying water into the air, the mist fanning out like a rooster tail. I came back down softly on the top of the falling water and bounced a little, then jumped off.

"How do I do that spray thingy?" she asked when I reached her again.

"One thing at a time," I said, laughing.

"Can't be that hard if you can do it."

"Just worry about staying upright first."

"Nothing to worry about," she said, pivoting into position.

"Push up when you feel it lift you," I said as the wave came in behind her. "Paddle now."

She drove her arms through the water. The wave picked her up, and she pushed herself up at the top, just like I told her. The board slid down the face, and her eyes got big, the drop and speed probably surprising her. She shuffled her feet, tilted backward, tried to correct, and tumbled face-first into the water.

I turned around so she wouldn't see me laughing.

"I know you're laughing," she yelled.

"No. Huh-uh."

"Screw you."

The laugh was gone by the time she reached my side.

"That was good," I said.

"Screw you again."

"I'm serious. Except for the part where you face-planted, you had it."

She pointed to the break line. "Go show off some more. I need to watch a couple more times."

I did as directed. For about fifteen minutes, I rode everything that came in, cutting and dropping, snapping and maneuvering. The fresh air and salt water felt good against my face. Everything that had been cluttering up my mind was gone. The ocean was always my cure all, cleansing me in every way. It never let me down.

Liz glided out to the line. "Okay, I think I've got it."

"After watching someone like me, you should have no problem."

"Whatever," she said.

I paddled in toward the shore, then turned back so I could watch as she came at me.

She missed the first, paddling too late, and it swept under her, leaving her behind. She got into the second, but fell over trying to get up. Ditto the third. And the fourth.

On the fifth, I could see she was pissed. She popped up at the top, her mouth a tight line of determination. Her knees bent with the drop, and she slid down smoothly. She followed it down the line and looked like she knew what she was doing.

As the wave cashed out, she thrust her fists into the air and fell into the water backward.

There was something in that moment, something in those raised fists and her determined look, in the ocean, that opened a door inside of me. Watching her, being with her, I felt like I was right where I belonged with whom I belonged. It occurred to me that Liz trumped all of the negative cards in my life. I hadn't ever felt that way that I could recall, and I didn't want that feeling to ever leave.

She emerged from the water about twenty feet away, her hair everywhere, those eyes gleaming in the shadowy sunlight, hands on her hips, waiting for my critique.

"Well?" she said, as impatient as ever.

My heart was thumping like a jackhammer. Right where I belonged with who I belonged.

"I love you," I said to her across the water.

She stared at me, her hands sliding off her hips. A small wave crashed into her, knocking her off balance for a moment. She regained her footing and waded awkwardly over to me, her board leashed to her ankle, dragging behind her.

She ran a hand through her hair, moving it away from her eyes and smoothing it back. "What did you say?"

The jackhammer was working overtime, and I felt like a high school kid again, embarrassed over a crush.

"I said, A-plus." I nodded toward the shore. "Let's head in."

I slid onto the board before she could object and paddled in, letting the tiny waves push me forward. I rolled off and squeezed my eyes shut as I submerged myself in the ocean.

I came up for air, and Liz was standing right in front of me.

"That's not what you said," she said.

The sun was a third gone, spraying pinks and yellows across the horizon.

I stood. "No, it wasn't."

"I heard what you said."

The water was cold around my feet, my toes digging into the sand. "Okay."

She moved her eyes away from me, looking down the shore. Beads of saltwater clung to her cheeks and neck. A sliver of her stomach was visible where her rash guard had ridden up. She pulled her hair around, gathered it at the bottom, and squeezed the water out.

She cut her eyes back to me. "You can't take that back, you know?"

I reached down and ripped the Velcro leash off my ankle and tossed it to the ground. "I don't want to."

"You say that now," she said, the green in her eyes bright. "But somewhere down the line you may want to. Something might change, and maybe you won't feel the same way."

High tide was coming in, and the water crashed a little higher against our legs.

"I don't think so, Liz," I said, as sure as I'd ever been about anything.

Her eyes held mine, probably waiting for me to look away, to see if what I'd said was impulsive or impetuous.

I didn't look away.

"Fine," she finally said.

"Fine?"

And standing there against the sunset, the pinks and yellows glowing against the blue and white of the water, Liz said to me, "I love you, too."

THIRTY

We went back to her place, cleaned ourselves up, and walked down to Peohe's for dinner.

Our conversation in the water had confirmed things between us. In reality, we weren't telling each other things we didn't already know. You spend that much time with someone in the way that we did and you just know. But saying it out loud had obliterated that invisible barrier that stayed up until each person came clean. An easiness and sense of permanency descended on me as we strolled to the harbor, holding hands.

The hostess recognized Liz and placed us at a table near the immense window overlooking Glorietta Bay. The lights of the downtown high-rises were gleaming in the early evening darkness.

We ordered a bottle of Merlot and our food, and Liz was looking at me a little funny as she finished her first glass.

"What?" I asked.

"Nothing's really changed," she said, a faint pink sunburn on her cheeks. "But it feels like everything's changed."

"I agree."

"You think that will be a problem?"

"Only if we continue to analyze the hell out of it."

"Then let's not do that."

I picked up the wine bottle, held it out, and refilled her glass. "Agreed."

"Tell me about your day," she said.

I recounted my trip to the casino, my conversation with Carolina, and Miranda's arrival.

"Well, that's a load," she said when I finished. "Maybe I should hold off on what I have for you."

Our food arrived, and we were halfway through it before I responded.

"Tell me," I said.

She wiped her mouth with the linen napkin, dropped it back in her lap, and tented her elbows and hands over her plate. "I called the cop who handled Simington's case."

The ease and comfort from earlier began to slip away. "And?"

"Name is Asanti. Works out of Imperial Valley in El Centro. Seemed like a good guy. Gave me what he could, which wasn't much different than what we already knew."

I forked the last piece of salmon and shoved it in my mouth.

"The names of the two vics were Miguel Tenayo and Hernando Vasquez," she said. "On the record, he said they were both illegals and not a whole lot of effort went into the investigation."

"Off the record?"

"Vasquez's family is in El Centro."

I set down the fork, letting it clink against the plate. "Legally?"

She shook her head. "No. That's why he gave it to me off the record. A wife and two kids. He found them during his investigation. He knew that if he put that in the case report, INS would jump all over it." She pulled her elbows off the table and folded her arms across her chest. "Like I said, Asanti seemed like a good guy. They already lost a husband and father. He didn't see the point in making it worse."

I pushed my plate away, the food suddenly feeling heavy and uncomfortable in my stomach. A woman left without her husband and two boys without their father.

Thanks to Russell Simington.

My father.

"The way Asanti put the case together, Tenayo and Vasquez still owed part of the mule fee after they'd made it across," Liz said. "They were late in paying up. Simington was sent to punish them. Those details came from Simington himself. Tenayo had no family here, and Vasquez's wife said she knew nothing of the details of his coming across. They came across separately."

The black water rippled with silver outside the window. Anger was beginning to boil in my gut. It was one thing for a father to choose to stay outside of a family. It was another thing entirely to take away a man's chance to choose.

"I told Asanti we'd be out in the morning," Liz said.

I shifted my gaze from the water to her. "Thanks."

The check came, I paid, and we walked outside into the cool air.

Liz looked up at the sky. "It's supposed to get ugly the next few days. Lots of rain."

I grunted in response, unable to shake what she'd told me from my head.

We walked back up the street in silence, her hand warm in mine.

We were halfway up the walk to her house when I stopped.

"You don't have to go tomorrow," I said.

She stared at me, her eyes searching. "Do you not want me to go?"

"No, it's not that. But I don't want you to feel like you have to."

Liz gripped my hand a little tighter and pulled me toward the front door. She fished her keys out of her pocket and unlocked the door, then turned to me.

"When you said earlier that you loved me, I said that maybe something would come up and maybe you'd change your mind. You disagreed."

"And I meant that, Liz."

"I know." She placed her hands lightly on my chest. "There is nothing that I'm going to hear about Russell Simington that is going to change *my* mind as to how I feel about you."

It was the second time Liz had said something like that to me, and yet I couldn't disentangle myself from what Simington was and who I was. It wasn't that I didn't believe her. But there was this continued nagging in the back of my mind that something ugly would emerge and everyone would look at me differently.

Her hands moved from my chest to around my neck. "Now. Earlier, I didn't get to see you change."

I pushed Simington out of my mind, refusing to let him ruin the rest of my evening, and focused on the woman I now freely admitted was the most important person in my life. "Your loss," I said.

"Care to come in and show me what I missed out on?"

It was an offer I couldn't—and didn't—refuse.

THIRTY-ONE

To find El Centro, you head east on I-8 and push through the El Cajon valley, the mountains of Alpine and Julian, and descend into the desert-covered region that reaches toward Arizona. It has become the furthest suburb of San Diego—if a community one hundred miles away can be considered a suburb—home to not only bedroom commuters but Mexican immigrant families that like the nearly visible proximity to their homeland. Ten minutes to the east and you are in Arizona. But ten minutes south and you enter the poverty-stricken zone of Mexicali.

I'd left a message for Miranda, letting her know where the towels were, that she was welcome to anything in the fridge and that I was sleeping elsewhere. But I hadn't slept. I tossed and turned all night and Liz had recognized my impatience at waiting for the day to begin. She volunteered to drive, and we took the circular off-ramp into El Centro at nine on the button.

We pulled up in front of a small, square building about a mile down Central Avenue. Letters spelling out "El Centro Police Department" were lined above two dirty glass doors at the entrance.

"Looks deserted," I said.

"Not a huge department," Liz said, shutting off the engine. "Asanti is the only detective. Four full-time officers, two part-time, and a dispatcher. Not much help for all the crap out here."

I nodded. The ease with which one could come and go to Mexico had created a sort of safe haven for crime. Steal a car and drive across the border. Buy your drugs and drive across the border. Kill someone and disappear across the border. But the tax base, even with the influx of new money brought from the folks making the drive to jobs in San Diego, wasn't enough to provide the protection and enforcement the area needed. Residents couldn't afford to move closer, though, as the cost of living grew exponentially each mile closer to the coast.

We entered through the glass doors. The crescent-shaped reception desk was empty. We walked past it and found a man sitting at a beaten-up desk in a large room that housed several other desks, all empty.

He looked up, his brown eyes rimmed with tired, red veins. "Help you?"

"We're looking for Detective Asanti," Liz said.

"I'm him," he said, rising out of the chair. "You must be Santangelo."

He was maybe six feet tall and thin like a stick of gum. A red tie was sloppily knotted at the neck of a short-sleeve white work shirt. Grey slacks revealed permanent wrinkles in the thighs, and his black leather shoes were dusty and well worn.

He extended his hand to Liz. "Aurelio Asanti."

"I'm Liz," she said, and they shook. Liz looked at me. "This is Noah Braddock."

We shook hands.

He looked at Liz. "I called Lucia Vasquez. She was not anxious to see us, but she agreed."

"Thank you," Liz said.

He shifted his eyes to me. "I cannot promise that she will have anything to tell you. And I would appreciate it if you would not press her on questions she does not wish to answer."

"I don't want to upset her," I said.

He gave a curt nod, then held out a hand in the direction we'd come in. "Let's go, then."

Asanti drove a late model Crown Victoria that looked as if it had just been pulled out of the detail garage. The white paint gleamed in the sunlight, and the windows were so clean they were barely visible. Liz rode in front, and I stretched out in the expansive backseat.

We drove south, through the downtown area of buildings in disrepair, boarded-up store fronts, and sidewalks overgrown with weeds.

"Makes you want to consider moving, right?" Asanti asked, a disappointed smile on his face in the rearview mirror.

"Not so much," I said. "How did you end up here?"

"I didn't end up here," he said, no animosity in his voice. "It's where I grew up. My parents came across two weeks before I was born. I went to school over in Tucson, but other than those four years, I've never lived anywhere else."

"Why did you come back?" Liz asked.

"Even though it's growing, I know most of the families here," he said. "Most started out as mine did. Entering illegally and finding a way to stay. Some people would say different, but I was fortunate to be born here, and I am grateful for that. Working in the community where I was raised and with my friends, this is where I'm comfortable."

We crossed back under the interstate, and Asanti turned left, pointing us toward a group of ranch houses in the distance.

Asanti glanced in the mirror. "Mr. Simington lived here for a while."

I met his eyes, but didn't say anything.

"Many folks involved in the smuggling arrangements live here," he said. "It's convenient. Close to the international border, with highways that will take you west, east, and north as soon as you cross."

"Did you know him before you arrested him?" I asked.

Asanti nodded. "I did. Like I said, I know most everyone here. New guy moves in, you hear about it and you do some checking. When I saw his history, I introduced myself."

He stopped the car in front of a low-slung stucco one-story with a chain-link fence around the property. A rusted-out wagon and a tricycle missing a rear wheel were left for dead in the weeds that made up the yard.

Asanti shifted in the front seat and looked at me. "Funny thing was, we got along okay. He knew I was making a point in introducing myself. Didn't lie about who he was. Saw him around town, having coffee, eating lunch, those kinds of things. Always said hello." His eyes shifted to the house. "When the thing happened, he was the first person I went to. There was a car in his driveway that matched the description of one that had been seen near the killings. He never bothered to deny it. Like we both knew it was coming and he didn't feel like outrunning it. If I hadn't known he was in El Centro, I'm not sure he would've even hit the radar." Asanti shrugged and gestured at the house. "Come on."

I opened the door and slid out of the backseat, images of Simington flashing in my head like a slide show. With Carolina. In El Centro. In prison. They seemed like pictures randomly thrown together in a shoebox. Regardless of what I learned or what happened to him, I doubted I'd ever understand him.

Liz, Asanti, and I walked up the cracked sidewalk to the front of the house. The mesh on the screen door was torn in two places. Asanti rapped on the metal frame, the noise echoing down the quiet street.

The door opened, and a small woman in jeans and a yellow polo shirt appeared. She was drying her hands with a dish towel. Her shiny black hair was pulled back away from her face, showing immaculate dark skin and brown eyes. A small gold cross hung around her neck.

She and Asanti exchanged quick greetings in Spanish. She opened the door without smiling, her eyes moving past Liz to me. I felt her gaze stay on me as I stepped past her into the home.

The living room was small. A sofa against one wall, an old console television opposite it. Toys were piled in the corners. The carpeting was thin, but looked like it had just been vacuumed. A small kitchen table surrounded by four chairs was nestled in a corner next to the kitchen. A hallway split the kitchen and living room. The smell of burnt bacon floated in the air.

"Lucia Vasquez," Asanti said. "This is Ms. Santangelo and Mr. Braddock."

She nodded politely at each of us, still without a smile. "Good morning." Her voice was soft, with very little accent.

She gestured for us to sit on the sofa, and she pulled a chair away from the kitchen table and sat across from Liz and me. Asanti remained standing.

"Lucia, anything you tell them will stay between us," he said. "Nothing that you say can harm you. And if you do not wish to answer the questions, you do not have to." He turned to us. "Correct?"

Liz nodded.

I said, "Yes."

He nodded as if that was acceptable and then stepped away and took a seat at the kitchen table.

Liz looked at me.

"Mrs. Vasquez," I said, trying to organize my thoughts, "I am trying to learn whatever I can about the man that arranged to bring you and your family here."

She held my gaze. "We paid a man to come across."

"Did that man help you get here to El Centro?"

"Yes. We met him at our home in Mexico. He said if we can pay him, he will bring us to America."

"How did you meet him?"

"My husband," she said, her eyelids fluttering. "Hernando and Miguel met him in a restaurant in our town. They made the plans."

"You came here first?"

"Yes. Hernando wanted me to come with the boys first. To make sure we were safe. My sister lives here. We stayed with her for about six months. Then Hernando came with Miguel."

I thought of how frightening it must have been for her to travel with her sons and without her husband to a country she couldn't be sure wanted her. Lucia Vasquez was a brave woman.

"Detective Asanti told us that there was a problem with money. Was your husband unable to pay?" I asked.

A flicker of anger ran through her eyes, and she rubbed her hands together. "The man. He changed the money."

"Changed the money?"

She nodded, hard. "He told Hernando that it will cost five hundred dollars to come to America. Hernando paid him." Tears formed in the corners of her eyes. "But after he brings Hernando over, when he brings him to my sister's, he tells him that he must pay three hundred dollars. More. He did the same to Miguel." The anger flickered again. She wiped the tears from her eyes with her finger. "We did not have that. We spent everything we had to get all of us here."

I didn't want to ask questions that were going to bring back painful memories. But she had answers that I needed.

"When Hernando told him that you didn't have the money, what happened?" I asked.

She clasped her hands together and looked back up. She straightened herself in the chair. "Hernando told him he would get the money. The man gave him two days."

"But Hernando was unable to get the three hundred dollars?"

"He and Miguel, they each got two hundred dollars," she said, her words heavier with anger than sadness. "Our family and friends, they gave us what they could. Hernando thought this would be enough, and he tells the man that they will get the rest soon."

"But that wasn't enough?"

She shook her head slowly. "No. Hernando and Miguel, they got angry. They are afraid he will keep asking for money. For forever, you understand."

I did. Interest and extortion born out of fear.

"So Hernando and Miguel, they tell him no more. They tell him that they will go to the police and even go home to Mexico if they have to. But they will not pay him any more."

I glanced at Asanti. I wondered what he would've done if they had showed up at his station.

"That's when the other man showed up here." She paused, fixing her eyes on me. "The man that you look like."

I felt the blood rush to my face, like a kid who'd fallen down on the playground in front of all his friends.

"Wait," Liz said. "There were two men?"

Lucia nodded. "Yes. The man that killed Hernando and Miguel, I had never seen him before that night."

"Who was the other man?" I asked. "The man you paid."

"He had a funny name," she said, blinking as she tried to recall.

From down the hallway, young voices spilled out, hollering at each other. Two boys bounded into the living room and landed in pile at their mother's feet.

"Manuel! Rigo!" she said harshly. "We have guests."

The boys untangled themselves and stood. They looked to be six or seven years old, dressed in shorts and Chargers T-shirts. Both had the dark hair and dark skin of their mother. They looked at each other and giggled.

Lucia rattled off something in Spanish, and the giggling stopped. They looked at us.

"Sorry," the slightly taller one said.

"Sorry," the other one said.

Liz smiled. "It's okay, guys."

"We'll be done soon," Lucia told them. "Go back to your rooms."

They tore off toward the back of the house. I wondered if they knew what had happened to their father.

Lucia watched them go, then folded her hands in her lap.

"They're very handsome," Liz said.

Lucia forced a tiny smile. "Thank you. They are good boys."

Lucia turned to me. "The one that look like you. He was named Simmings. Something like that."

"Simington," I said, the name tasting sour as it came out of my mouth.

"Yes," she said. "And the man that we paid was named King, maybe? I remember he always wore a very crazy shirt."

"Crazy how?" I asked.

"Women dancing. Lots of colors."

A crazy shirt. I remembered the guy from the casino who Carter and I had exchanged words with.

And King sounded too close to the name Simington had given me to be a coincidence.

"Keene?" I said. "Landon Keene?"

She looked at me, then nodded slowly. "Yes. That is it."

THIRTY-TWO

"Do you know Keene?" I asked Asanti as we drove away from Lucia Vasquez's home.

"I know the name," Asanti said. "I've heard it mentioned in several different cases involving illegal transportation. Not in a good way. But I've never seen or spoken to him."

"What's your sense?" Liz asked.

"People are scared of him." Asanti turned back under the interstate and pointed us toward the station. "Most of these guys just use straight intimidation. It's the most effective tool to use against a person from another country. Immigrants fear the US authorities because they are worried about being sent back to Mexico, so they would rather deal with people like Keene or Simington."

I shifted in the seat. Every time I heard Simington's name it was like an unexpected pin prick that I couldn't dodge. In my eye.

"I think I met Keene," I said.

Liz turned around, and Asanti glanced in the rearview mirror.

I told them about the confrontation Carter and I had had with him on the casino floor.

Asanti pulled the car back into the police lot. We all got out.

"Not surprising," Asanti said.

"What's not?" I asked.

"Keene's presence in a casino."

"Why? Does he have a gambling problem?" I asked, thinking of Simington's debts.

"That I don't know," Asanti said, leaning against the trunk of the car. "But casinos are prime hunting grounds for people in his business."

"How do you mean?" Liz asked.

"Let's say Keene runs a ring of coyotes," Asanti explained. "He needs guys to run his cargo over the border. It's not the safest job in the world and not a position you send a resume for." A dour expression settled on his face. "Keene needs leverage to get people to work for him. He needs people who desperately need money."

"People with gambling problems," I said.

Asanti pushed off the trunk of the car. He pulled a handkerchief from his pocket and rubbed it over the spot he'd been leaning against, wiping away whatever minute smudge his weight might have created.

"Exactly," he said, putting the cloth back in his pocket. "They look for regulars, men who are sweating heavily as they lose. Guys who are there so often it's clear they aren't employed. They're not hard to spot. Their losses are piling up, and a guy like Keene offers them a way out. Quick cash for a little amount of work. Do the job, get the paycheck, and get right back to gambling. It's a dangerous, foolish way out, but a way nonetheless."

I thought back to Keene messing with the guy in the casino. At the time, the argument hadn't made sense, but after listening to Asanti, what had been going on seemed clear.

"Did you ever hear anything that put Simington and Keene together?" I asked.

"No," Asanti said. "But that doesn't mean it wasn't happening. Some things I get wind of, some I don't. Immigration isn't too gung-ho on bringing the local cops into their cases unless they have to."

"Do the casinos know what guys like Keene are doing?" Liz asked.

"They have to know," I said. "They've got cameras covering every centimeter. Nothing happens without their awareness. They wouldn't let some random guy hassle their customers."

"That could mean the casinos are involved," Liz said. "At least to some extent."

An image of Moffitt and his two thugs flashed through my head. I had no doubt they were capable of being involved in something like this.

"It would be risky for the casinos," Asanti said. "But I tend to agree with you. It could not happen without their knowledge."

"And if a casino owner is approving something, he's got a piece of the action," I said. "It would mean that a guy like Keene, one way or another, is working for the casino."

Liz and Asanti nodded in agreement, then Asanti glanced at his watch.

"I'm sorry," he said. "I've got a meeting. I need to go."

"Thank you for your help," Liz said.

"I'm sure you'll extend me the same courtesy someday," he said. He turned to me. "Good luck."

He walked back into the station, and we headed toward Liz's car.

"What do you think?" she asked.

One thing in particular had parked itself front and center in my thoughts, and I wasn't happy about it. It was like buying a new game and emptying all the pieces onto the table. Everything was there—I just needed someone to show me how to play.

THIRTY-THREE

Liz and I made the long drive back to San Diego, the silence punctured only occasionally by small talk that went nowhere. I knew I had to go back to San Quentin—Simington threw out Keene's name like a challenge, and I'd met it—and I couldn't think about anything else.

We crossed the bridge into Coronado, and Liz pulled her car behind my Jeep when we reached her place. I got out and the burst of salt air wafting in from the bay gave me a temporary sense of comfort.

Liz came around to me. "When are you going to go?" she asked, reading my mind.

"Tomorrow, I think," I said. "I have to arrange the visit, and I'm not sure how that works. I'll have to ask Miranda and I need to make sure she's settled at my place. But the sooner I get up there, the sooner I can talk to Simington."

"This is gonna sound like a dumb question," Liz said, brushing her hair away from her face. "But why are you doing this? I mean, Darcy's the one who hired you, and she's dead. You've already recognized that you can't get Simington off the row, and I don't even think that's what you want. Talking to Simington and staying in the middle of this might help solve Darcy's death, but . . ." She paused, thinking about her words. "I don't think that's your responsibility."

Liz was right. With Darcy dead, there was no reason to keep looking. Hell, Simington had been clear on not wanting any help. There was no one pushing me to keep going forward. But I couldn't get past the fact that Simington had thrown out Keene's name. There had to be a reason for that.

"I think it's just that it's him," I said, leaning against the car and watching the water. "I know he killed Vasquez and Tenayo. He deserves to die. That's not going to change." The bay sparkled under the late morning sun. "But he's my father. Before he goes, I want to be clear on what he did. And I want to know why. Not for him. For me."

Liz snaked her arm around mine and pressed up against me. "I'm not telling you not to do it. I'm not. But knowing why he did it may hurt more than not knowing at all."

"I know," I said, shifting my weight against the car.

She was right. The reasons, if Simington did talk, wouldn't make sense to me. There was nothing he could say to me that would justify what he did. But now that I had connected with him—no matter the bizarre fashion—I felt an urge I couldn't push away. I needed to learn as much about him as I could.

"Maybe he can tell me something that will help with Darcy," I said. "He acted like he didn't want her help, but I don't think he disliked her. Maybe he can do one good thing before he dies."

Liz's hand slid down my arm, and she folded her fingers into mine. "Do you really think he'll do that?"

A bank of gray clouds drifted in front of the sun, turning the bright glare on the water into a black shadow.

"Probably not," I said, squeezing her hand, glad to have something to hold onto. "But what else do I have?"

WEEK TWO

THIRTY-FOUR

I spent the night with Liz and got up early the next morning. I told her I'd call to let her know what I was doing, then headed back to Mission Beach to talk to Miranda and make my plans to go back to San Francisco. I parked a couple blocks from my place and walked up the boardwalk, watching the clouds get darker and grayer over the ocean. Liz had mentioned rain was in the forecast, and it looked to be only a couple hours away.

Carter was on my patio, staring through the slider into my place like he couldn't see what was inside.

"What the hell are you doing?" I asked as I stepped over the wall.

"Dude," he said, jabbing his finger toward the door. "You've got a wiccan in there."

"A wiccan?"

"She's dressed in black, has the personality of a pissed-off cobra, and is about as charming as cancer."

"Oh. That's Miranda," I said.

"I went in to get something to eat," he said, still staring at the door. "She came out of nowhere. Like a puff of smoke or something. Told me to get out. I was afraid she'd sic her flying monkeys on me if I didn't."

I looked in through the door. Miranda was sitting on the sofa watching television, paying us no attention.

"She's harmless," I said.

He glanced at me, skeptical. "Wiccans aren't to be messed with, dude. Spells, curses, shit like that."

"Come on," I said, opening the slider. "I've got some garlic in the fridge."

"Garlic is vampires, man," he whispered. "Witches are a whole different thing."

"How would you know?" I asked.

He moved in right behind me as if we were two kids walking into a haunted house. "I watch the Discovery Channel. Trust me."

Miranda looked up as we stepped into the living room. "Well, well. Nice of you to finally show up." She looked past me to Carter. "And you brought a pet."

Carter walked slowly around the dining room table and into the corner of the room, so that he was as far away from her as possible.

"Miranda, this is Carter," I said. "Carter, Miranda."

Carter stared at her like she was a giant spider. Miranda smiled back like she was about to sink her fangs into him.

"Gorilla-boy startled me this morning," she said. "Thanks for the tip on the towels and the food. I slept in your bed. When I came out this morning, he was lurking."

"I was not lurking," he said.

"You're lurking right now," she said, raising a blackened eyebrow. "I'm fairly certain you've been lurking your whole life. It seems to be in your nature."

Carter started to say something, then stopped and shot me a look wanting my help. It was rare that anyone could get him off balance, and I was enjoying it.

"She doesn't bite," I said to him.

"You don't know that," Miranda said, her licorice-colored lips curling into a you-have-no-idea-what-I'm-capable-of sneer.

Carter took a step back and bumped into the wall.

"Anyway," I said, "I need to go back to San Francisco."

The sneer faded from her face. "Why?"

"I'm gonna go talk to Simington again."

"What about Darcy?" she asked.

"The police here are on it. There's not much I can do. And I might actually be able to get some information from Simington that could help them."

She tucked her knees beneath her and leaned against the back of the sofa. "What kind of info?"

"I'm not sure yet. But remember when I asked you about a guy named Landon Keene? I know who he is now." I turned to Carter, who was still wedged into the corner. "Remember that guy in the casino?"

He reluctantly pulled his eyes off Miranda and moved them to me. "That asshole in the shitty shirt?"

"Yep. Him."

"Who is he?" Miranda asked.

I gave them a brief version of what Liz and I had learned in El Centro.

"So Simington worked for Keene?" Miranda asked.

"It sounds like they worked together in some capacity," I said. "I'm just not sure how. That's what I want to know."

Miranda slid off the sofa and stood. She was wearing a black T-shirt, cut above her waist, that had "GOOD GIRL" written in white letters across the chest. Stainless steel gleamed in several painful looking piercings around her exposed navel.

"No offense," she said. "But I don't see how that's gonna help figure out what happened to Darcy."

"It may not," I said. "I'm going to go talk to him, though. Can you set up the visit like you did last time?"

Annoyance rippled across her face. "Finding out who killed Darcy is more important to me than setting up a reunion with your daddy. I know you've got issues, but I came down here to figure out what happened to Darcy, not to be your secretary."

"I'm not asking you to be my secretary," I said, resisting the urge to yank on one of those metal bars in her stomach. "If you don't want to make the call, fine. Tell me what I need to do."

"Do you really think the cops are working hard on Darcy's murder?" she asked. "Please. They've probably got fifteen other cases just like hers." She folded her arms across her chest. "No. We do something about Darcy first before you go back to San Francisco."

I felt my teeth grind together and the muscles in my jaw twitch as I tried to keep from picking her up, carrying her down to the ocean, and drowning her little gothic ass. I looked at Carter.

He held his hands up like he wanted no part of her.

Which, unfortunately for him, gave me an idea.

"How about this, then," I said to Miranda. "You set up the visit with Simington, I go to San Francisco, and you and Carter stay here and do some interviewing."

"What?" Carter said, his voice shooting up about three octaves. Miranda and I both looked at him. He cleared his throat and tried for his normal voice. "What?"

"Start checking with the neighbors and see if you can't find out more about the guy who was seen here the night of Darcy's murder," I said. "You know the people who live around here. They'll talk to you. They won't talk to Miranda if she's alone."

Miranda nodded. "Alright. I can live with that." She looked at Carter and the sneer from earlier reappeared. "How about you, King Kong? Think you can ask a few questions without sounding like your nuts are caught in the drawer?"

Carter's cheeks reddened. I wasn't sure I'd ever had the pleasure of witnessing that before.

"As long as you keep your cauldron and broom away from me," he said, trying to save a little face.

She sauntered around the table toward him. He pressed himself further into the wall, which only made it easier for Miranda to corner him.

She looked him up and down, then placed her index finger on his chest. "Don't you worry, sweetheart. I've got other plans for you."

His eyes widened.

She let her finger fall down to his stomach, gave a short, harsh laugh, and disappeared into my bedroom.

THIRTY-FIVE

I caught an early-evening flight to San Francisco, and by the time I'd landed in the mist and fog, Miranda had left a message on my cell phone telling me that she arranged a visit with Simington the next morning at nine. No word on how she and Carter were getting along.

After renting a car, I spent the night at a hotel near the airport, watching TV in between useless fits of sleep. The anxiety of the entire situation was doing its best to wrestle me to the ground, and I was doing a poor job of fighting it off.

I crawled out of bed at six and did an hour of running on the treadmill in the hotel's fitness room. I showered, dressed, checked out, and made the drive up to San Quentin under a wet, gray sky.

The guard at the gate found my name on the visitation list and seated me at the same window as before. Simington appeared in the yellow coveralls, his hair damp and slicked back, the glasses gone from his face this time.

"Surprised you're back," he said as he sat down.

I saw the letters of my name tattooed on his wrist again, snagging me like a piece of cloth on a nail. I ripped my eyes away.

"You and Landon Keene worked together," I said. "I'm not sure how. My guess is you worked for him. He handled the money and the business." I paused. "You handled the killing."

Laughter drifted in from somewhere behind me. It seemed heavy and awkward and out of place.

Simington didn't move. His expression didn't change.

"Am I right?" I asked.

"Does it matter?" he responded.

"You were the one who threw his name out there," I said. "You wouldn't have done that if he didn't matter."

Simington looked away. I knew I was right. I hadn't said it to Liz when she'd asked me why I was doing this, but I felt like there had to be a reason for Simington to have thrown Keene's name out to me. He could have said nothing and let me walk away. But he chose to give me a crumb.

Simington let his gaze come back to me. "You meet Keene?"

I nodded.

"You tell him who you were?"

"Does it matter?" I said.

The corners of his mouth tightened. It was as much emotion as I'd seen from him in either visit. But I could tell he was agitated. And I took some juvenile pride in having splintered his exterior.

"Did you tell him who you were?" he repeated.

"I didn't know it was him when I met him," I said. "But I got the sense he knew who I was."

The corners tightened again and the green in his eyes went a little darker. "Where did you meet him?"

"Bareva Casino. I met the casino operator, Ben Moffitt, too."

Simington folded his hands together and several of his knuckles cracked. He brought his eyes back to me.

"Don't go back there," he said, his voice dropping an octave.

"Why?"

"Because I said so."

I leaned forward, my face close to the window, the anger washing through me like a dam had burst.

"Are you fucking kidding me?" I said. "Because you said so?" My neck burned, the blood working its way up my body. "Don't *ever* speak to me like you're my father again. Ever. *We* don't have that kind of relationship."

We stared at each other through the plexiglass. I realized I was breathing like I'd just run a five-minute mile. I pulled back and tried to catch my breath.

Simington looked cool and collected. He unfolded his hands, seemed unsure of what to do with them, and then put them back together.

"I shouldn't have given you his name," he said. "It doesn't mean anything."

"Why?" I asked, my breathing returning to a normal cadence. "Because I learned what you did with him? You think I thought you were in here for littering?"

"Nothing good is going to come from messing with Keene," he said.

"Surprise. What about Moffitt?"

Simington licked his lips slowly, then shook his head. "Him either."

"But you gave me Keene's name, I found him, and now I'm here. You owe me."

"I don't owe you anything, Noah," he said. "Remember? We don't have that kind of relationship."

Throwing my words back in my face. Clever. And effective.

"Darcy's dead," I said, trying a different path.

"The lawyer?"

I nodded.

His eyes shifted away for a moment, and he glanced down at his hands. He pulled them apart, laid them flat on the small overhang in front of him, and looked at me. "That's too bad."

"Yeah, it is," I said. "She didn't deserve it. She was trying to help you."

"I didn't want her help."

"And, yet, she tried anyway. So maybe you don't owe me. But you at least owe her."

A guard appeared behind Simington. He stood there for a moment, just checking to make sure things were okay. We both watched him until he moved on.

"I figured Keene would be dead," Simington said.

"What?"

"When I gave you his name. I figured he'd be dead by now," he said, pinching the bridge of his nose.

"Why?"

"Because he's a piece of shit, and I thought someone would've punched his ticket by now. I wanted to make sure he was in the ground." He took his hand away from his face. "You're in danger."

"I can handle myself."

He laughed and shook his head. "You think because you have a PI license you're tough? Because maybe you get in a few scrapes here and there? That makes you tough?" Simington leaned closer to the window. "Keene is a different kind of tough, Noah. Not your kind."

I shifted in the seat, uncomfortable under his hard watch. "You still haven't explained your relationship with Keene."

He grunted, pushing back from the window. "You got it right. I worked for him. I killed those two men in the desert because he told me to."

"Why?"

Simington stared at me like he was trying to make a decision. Sitting under his look was uncomfortable, but I didn't turn away. I refused to be the one who blinked. And in that hard, unflinching stare, I could see it—all the years of what he'd done and the time in prison. There wasn't much that could reach or scare Russell Simington.

"Why?" I repeated.

And then a tiny crack appeared in his expression, his hardened features softening for just a moment.

"Because if I hadn't," he said, "you and Carolina were going to die."

THIRTY-SIX

Simington rubbed a finger over the tattoo of my name on his wrist. "Your mother was smart to tell me to get lost when she did. I wasn't a complete disaster when you were born, but I was heading in that direction."

I took a deep breath. I knew I was about to hear some things I'd wondered about my whole life. I wasn't sure I was ready for it.

"Don't get the wrong idea," he said, an empty smile on his face. "I was never into anything good. It was just varying degrees of bad. Didn't know any different. And I was good at what I did."

"Which was?"

"I enforced." He laughed, shaking his head. "I always liked that word. Almost made it sound legit. I was hired muscle. Threatened, intimidated, beat the shit out of people." He paused. "Sometimes more."

The glass between us was cloudy, smudged. I wanted to wipe it clean so I could see his face clearly.

"Keene and I ran in the same circles," he said. "When all you do is the wrong thing, you get hooked into the bad guy underground network. We were both in it. We had done some jobs together, some small-time stuff." The expression on his face darkened, and he folded his thick arms across his chest. "Then he got something on me."

"Your gambling?" I asked.

He raised an eyebrow, surprised, then slowly nodded. "Nice work. Yeah. The gambling. I was shit deep in debt, and it was growing by the hour. I couldn't stop it."

"You could've stopped gambling."

"Please. You've proved already that you aren't stupid. All the clichés about gamblers? They all applied to me. I always thought my next big play was the one that would right the ship. And it wasn't like

I was going to get a job to pay off the debt." The empty smile reappeared. "A real job, anyway."

"What did you do before the casinos and Keene?" I asked for my own curiosity.

He shrugged. "Nothing you'd wanna hear about. Like I said. Hired muscle. Some of it was legit, some of it wasn't. Same shit, different places. Not like I was punching a clock. Money was always good and when you aren't afraid of much, you can always find work. I collected for dealers. Did some protection work for them. Pickup and delivery. I tried construction, but it didn't take." He shifted his weight. "I was better at destruction."

That sounded about right.

"Not like I ever put a resume together, Noah," he said. "The work I did, you don't need one. You meet people in bars and your name gets around and you hang around in the wrong crowds. That's your resume. I started right out of high school, delivering boosted cars, and it just grew. Always had cash in my pocket, never had a schedule, and I was good at it. Hard to believe you could get by doing that shit for thirty years, but I managed alright. And if I hadn't started gambling, I'd still be doing it."

"How'd that start?"

He laughed, shook his head. "Simple hundred dollar bet on a Lakers game one night. I won. Wasn't a big deal that night, but, man. It flipped a switch."

I took a deep breath, settled my thoughts.

"Okay. How did Keene play in?" I asked.

"He was employed by the casino," Simington said. "By Moffitt. They extended me some credit lines—probably because they knew I'd never be able to get even, I was so far in. So they let me fall a little further. When it got pretty obvious that I wasn't getting out of the hole anytime soon, they cut me off and told me I owed them."

Simington leaned back in the chair and glanced over his shoulder as another guard did a walk-by. "I did some simple stuff first. Collecting and what not. Enough that I thought we were square."

"Wait. Was Keene running a smuggling operation?"

Simington shook his head. "Yeah. Moffitt lets him scout his casinos for guys who are desperate for cash, maybe in over their heads, deep enough that they're willing to do something illegal."

"Drive people over the border."

He nodded. "In return, Moffitt gets a percentage of Keene's operation."

"Why would Moffitt want in? That's a huge risk for nickels and dimes."

Simington shrugged. "I don't know. Moffitt and Keene were tight. Keene ran a lot, though. Wasn't just nickels and dimes. He was making some serious money."

I filed that away for later thought. "Okay. You thought you were square."

"Right. I thought I was done. My debt was square and I'd curbed the gambling. I was picking up odd jobs, looking for something steady. But then Keene told me I had one last job."

"Vasquez and Tenayo?" I said.

"Names all sound the same to me."

I looked away, thinking it was a bad idea to try to punch my hand through the window to choke him.

"Hey." He leaned toward the window again. "Wasn't my business to know their names."

"What a professional," I said, turning back to him.

"I was a professional," he said, his eyes narrowing. "Because I told him I wouldn't do it."

"Why not?"

"Because it was a bullshit job and I knew it," he said. "I knew the two Mexicans had probably paid Keene and he was just being the vicious asshole he loves being. I had no problem collecting from guys who owed. But I didn't make it my business to take out guys who had paid their debts. I don't know if Keene did it on a regular basis—knowing him he probably did—but I didn't want any part of that." He laid his palms flat on the counter beneath the glass. "So I said no."

"But you did kill them," I said. "You admitted that. So what happened?"

Simington took a deep breath and leaned away from the window, uncertainty slipping onto his face for the first time in my two visits. His fingers went to the tattoo again for a moment, like my name might give him something. It made me want to rip the letters off his skin.

"I told Keene no," he said. "He could take those guys out himself if he wanted it done. Figured the worst he would do was come after me. I had no problem with that. I wasn't afraid of him because I was square and thought I was out from under him." He hesitated. "But he went a different route."

He ran a hand through his hair, pulling at it, the skin tightening across his forehead. "Showed up two days after I told him no. Laid a piece of paper down in front of me. Had Carolina's address and yours. Then he laid down a picture of each of you." He shook his head, the anger bubbling in his eyes. "I never talked about either of you, but he found out."

The whispers from the other windows filtered over the dividers, jumbled words and phrases. I wondered if anyone else was speaking with their father or having an even remotely similar conversation.

"I decked him," Simington said, a corner of his mouth rising up. "But he just laughed. The message was clear. Do the job or he'd have someone do the job on both of you. We both knew he had me. I went to El Centro the next day and got it done."

"Why didn't you tell anyone this when you were arrested?" I asked. "Why not tell the cops about Keene?"

"Because I knew if I dragged him in, he'd have someone on the outside get to you and Carolina," he said. "Only way to protect you was to keep my mouth shut and take what came my way. And as I've already told you," he said, angling toward the window, "I'm alright with all of it. I'm not here just because of what I did for Keene. This is my reward for a lifetime of work."

I didn't know what to think of him. What he'd done was despicable. There was no way to dress it up. And, yet, because I was essentially part of the excuse for his actions, I felt there was something oddly honorable about his story. He'd chosen me and I'd gone a lifetime thinking he'd never done that. It was both comforting and disconcerting.

"So you never contested your sentence because you knew it might bring Keene's involvement to light?" I said.

He nodded. "First time Darcy came here, took me about two minutes to realize that if I gave her anything, she'd dig it out. She wasn't going to go through the motions. She actually thought she could overturn the conviction." He rubbed a hand across his jaw. "Giving her your name was a way to pacify her. I didn't figure on you getting involved. I just assumed that you wouldn't want anything to do with me and would send her on her way."

Remembering Darcy in the ocean that day we met, I knew sending her on her way was exactly what I should have done. She'd still be alive, and I wouldn't have been sitting in San Quentin with a man who was taking a power saw to my life.

"I swear, I thought Keene would either be dead or you wouldn't be able to find him. Guy has to have about a million enemies and I thought something or someone would've gotten to him by now," Simington said. "It was a stupid mistake on my part. I'm sorry."

"Am I right in thinking he killed Darcy?" I asked.

"Yeah. He must've gotten wind of her taking on my case. I'm sure he keeps an eye on me, waiting for them to strap me in."

I was unnerved by the way he talked about his own death with such detachment.

"I'm taking him down, then," I said.

Simington shook his head. "Not worth it, Noah. She's gone, and that's too bad. But it's my fault because I started this chain reaction. It's not your problem to solve." His eyes hardened. "Best thing you can do is to step away from this now. It's what's best for you and your mother."

It may have been what was best for everyone, but I didn't care. Keene had killed Darcy and dumped her in my apartment. Maybe he hadn't killed Vasquez and Tenayo, but he'd been a part of it.

"Someone has to fight for Darcy," I said. "I'm taking him down."

"There's only one way to take him down, Noah," Simington said.

"What's that?"

Simington leaned closer to the window, the smudges and finger-prints distorting his face. "Kill him."

THIRTY-SEVEN

I set Simington's advice aside for the moment. "You need a new lawyer."

"No," Simington said, shaking his head. "I don't. I'm fine."

"This kind of information could change your sentence," I said.

"We already went through that. I did what I did, I'm going to take the punishment, and I'm alright with it."

He spoke as though he were serving a week-long detention rather than being executed. No matter how I felt about him, that didn't make sense to me.

"Why?" I asked.

"Why what?"

"Why are you so comfortable with dying?"

Chair legs scraped the floor on the other side of the room, echoing off the walls. We stared at each other for a few moments. I wasn't going to say anything until he answered the question.

"You're a good guy, aren't you, Noah?" he finally said.

I shrugged, not knowing how to answer.

"No, you are," he said, smiling. "I can tell. The fact that you're here, the fact that you found Keene, and the fact that you want justice for what happened to Darcy all tell me that."

I adjusted how I was sitting in the chair, the seat back suddenly feeling too hard.

"And I know what Carolina's like," he continued. "Your mother, I screwed that up, okay? I had a chance to actually have a decent life with her and I shot it all to hell. She was one of the few good things I ever ran across and like always, I fucked it up. She has her faults, but bottom line, she's a good person. It's natural that she would've passed that on to you."

That was difficult to hear. I chose to think that my personality traits evolved in a vacuum instead of having been passed down from people I was embarrassed by.

Simington pointed his index finger at his chest. "I'm not a good person. I've never been a good person. My parents were not good people, so it came easily for me."

I wondered about the grandparents I'd never known. "Are they still alive?"

"No, and the world is better for it," he said. "My old man died when I was fifteen. Shot in the chest during a burglary. And my mother passed on about ten years ago. Heart attack. All the stress of lying and stealing from people finally caught up to her." He paused. "You are better off never having met them."

My genetic hit streak continued.

"I have never wanted to be a good person," he said. "It never occurred to me. I didn't mind hurting people if it got me what I needed. I was looking out for myself, and fuck the rest of the world."

He pointed the index finger at me now. "You care that Darcy was killed. Even in here, with the chance to tell you that it matters to me, I can't. Because it doesn't. I'm sorry she's dead, but it doesn't affect me. If I were on the outside, her death would be about as important to me as the weather."

I leaned forward, my elbows resting on my knees.

"But when I killed those two men in the desert, I knew I was done," Simington said. "I'd crossed my own pathetic line. I hated myself for doing it. And I knew I couldn't change myself. I'm too lazy. There wouldn't be enough in it for me to do that." He hesitated, his eyes staring right through me. "I am in the best place for me, headed toward what is the best thing for me. Staying here and accepting my fate is the only good thing I will ever do."

He spoke with such conviction, I knew his words weren't a ploy to garner sympathy. He'd arrived at a truth in his life, no matter how brutal it seemed to the outside world. Even with my emotions twisted into an impossible knot, I knew it wasn't my place to talk him out of it.

"I'm serious, Noah," he said. "This isn't your fight. It's not worth it. You need to stay away from Keene."

I stood. "I appreciate the warning."

Irritation coiled in his face. "Did you hear anything I said?"

"Yeah. I heard it all."

"Then drop this. All of this. Darcy, me, and Keene. Let it go today." He stared at me through the window. "Go back to your life. Do the right thing."

I walked out of San Quentin, but I had no idea what the right thing was.

THIRTY-EIGHT

Detective Ken Kenney held out a stick of gum outside San Quentin.

"No thanks," I said, trying to brush past him.

He stepped just close enough to slow me down so he could walk with me. He shoved the gum into his mouth. "Been a lot of your father's old friends checking in on him lately."

"Excuse me?"

"He's had a lot of visitors in the last day or so," he said. "How is he?"

I wondered if Kenney slept in the parking lot. "He's wonderful."

"His time is slowly eroding," he said. "Certainly that is affecting him."

"Go ask him yourself."

He laughed, but it was hollow and jagged. "Next time I see him, it'll be only to make sure he's no longer breathing."

"Good to have something to hold onto," I said as we reached my rental car.

"Perhaps then I'll be able to let go." Kenney cleared his throat. "Heard about Ms. Gill. I'm sorry."

"I'll bet."

"Regardless of my wishes for your father, I did not want to see anyone else hurt by their involvement with him." He pulled the gum out of his mouth and tossed it away. "She told you why I'm hanging around, correct?"

"She did."

"You ask him? About my nephew?"

I looked away and shook my head.

"You should. Be interesting to see what he says."

I felt caught in the middle, but I wasn't sure why. Simington may have been my father, but it was a title on a piece of paper and nothing else. Yet, when Kenney spoke to me, I felt defensive.

"What happened?" I asked.

He stared at me for a moment, then leaned against the passenger door of the rental, his arms folded across his chest. "Jacob was a screw-up."

"Your nephew?"

He nodded. "My sister had a helluva time with him. Couldn't get him pointed down the right road. He was just determined to go the wrong way. But that doesn't make it any easier, you know?"

I did.

"As clichéd as it sounds, Jacob fell in with the wrong crowd," Kenney said, his voice not as confident as it had been before. "Kept getting nicked here and there. Some theft, an assault, that sort of stuff. Not big time, but it was building." He ran a hand across his jaw. "Started doing some work for a guy who runs a backroom operation."

"Gambling?"

"Yeah. Poker games, horses, sports. The guy's been doing it forever, and to be honest, so are a lot of others. It's not a high priority to quash it all."

I believed that.

"Jacob stole from the guy. Five large," Kenney said, sounding like he'd bit into something that tasted awful. "Stupid, stupid move."

The story fell into place. "And the guy hired Simington to punish him," I said.

Kenney nodded. "Sure. It's what they do. Let anybody steal from you and your credibility with your bettors goes to shit. He had to take care of Jacob."

I shivered against the breeze that brushed across the parking lot.

"Simington was a pro. He came in and did what he was paid to do." He glanced at me. "He did it, Mr. Braddock. There is no doubt. He covered his tracks, and we couldn't get him. But he killed Jacob."

We let that hang between us.

"Jacob was not a good kid. But he was my nephew, and I don't believe anyone deserves to die like that," he said. "That's why I am preoccupied with your father."

It was like another kick to the shins.

"I'm sorry," I said. "I don't know what to say."

Kenney nodded. "Thank you. And I am sorry about Ms. Gill. We were on opposite sides, but I didn't wish her harm." He paused. "May I ask you a question?"

"What?"

"Have you hired another attorney?"

"He doesn't want one."

He nodded, satisfied. Then he looked at me in a strange way.

"What?" I asked.

"I had you all wrong."

"How's that?"

"Family member appears here, in this situation, they are usually desperate. Desperate to figure out a way to stop the train. But I don't see that in you."

I pulled the keys out of my pocket. "What do you see, Detective?"

Kenney stepped away from the car. "I see someone who's really confused."

"I always look that way."

He made a face and shook his head. "Funny, but I don't believe that." His eyes hardened. "Be clear on one thing, Mr. Braddock. There's nothing to be confused about. Russell Simington is as bad as they come." He waved a hand in the direction of the prison. "And this is where he belongs."

THIRTY-NINE

As my plane descended half an hour late into San Diego, thick rain clouds bounced us around, and lightning was visible out the windows when we touched down.

I was walking through the terminal, getting ready for the wet sprint to my Jeep, when I felt someone fall in step next to me.

"Shitty weather we're having, huh?" Landon Keene said, smiling.

I stopped, unable to hide my surprise.

Keene's smile grew. "Welcome home." He nodded toward the parking lot. "You wanna keep walking? I saw your Jeep out there."

A subtle message that he knew what I was driving. A surge of adrenaline kicked into gear.

"Sure," I said, trying to regain a little composure. "You can stand right behind it, and I'll throw it in reverse."

He laughed louder than necessary, tossing his head back like I'd told him the funniest joke he'd ever heard. His laugh died off, and he shook his head. "Sounds like your pop's been telling you some stories about me."

He was doing a terrific job of sticking his finger on my buttons.

"What the fuck do you want?" I asked.

"Just wanted to make sure you made it home okay. That trip from San Fran can be a tricky one."

The subtlety was gone.

"I made it just fine," I said.

Keene nodded. "Good, good, my man. Hope nothing will be waiting at home for you this time." He winked.

I stepped in closer, looking down at him. "I'm not some degenerate gambler, Keene. I will take you outside, break off each of your limbs, and set the rest of you on fire."

Keene stepped back, not because he was intimidated but so I could see his face. "All in good time, my man." He snapped his fingers, like he'd just remembered something. "By the way. Your mother is looking excellent these days."

My right hand curled into a fist, and I set my feet to throw a punch. But I knew what he was doing, and I didn't want him to win this battle. I forced my hand to unclench.

"Thanks for the update," I said. "I'll tell her that."

The smile drifted off his face, and he couldn't force the fake laugh. It looked like my refusal to engage had confused him.

An announcement came over the PA. Something about a flight delayed due to the weather. Neither of us paid attention, caught in a staring match.

"Amazing what a guy will tell someone when he's facing the death penalty," I said, turning the tables.

Irritation flashed across Keene's face.

"I mean, nobody wants to take their guilt to the grave," I continued. "Have to unload things, you know? Things like gambling, smuggling. Killing." I shrugged. "Guys even feel compelled to name names."

It was like I had transferred my anger right into his body. The relaxed, confident demeanor he had arrived with was gone.

"Careful, kid," he said, his voice much harder than before. "You don't want to step into this."

I threw my hands up like I was confused. "Step into what? I thought we were just talking."

"Worst thing you can do is talk," Keene said, shuffling a little closer. "You know what's good for you, kid, you better forget you ever heard dear old dad's voice in the pen."

"Why's that? Worried about something? Maybe I should ask Ben Moffitt about it."

Keene shook his head like I was brain damaged. "Only time I'm warning you, kid. Stay out of it."

"And if I don't?"

He took a couple of steps away from me, heading for the exit, the smile creeping back onto his face. "Then things are gonna start blowing up in your face."

FORTY

Keene had gotten into my head.

As I drove away from the airport, sheets of rain falling across the windshield like a dam in the sky had burst, I was no longer sure of what I needed to do.

I spent the night wrestling with that and awoke the next morning to torrents of rain. I grabbed a jacket for the first time in forever, ignored Miranda snoring on the couch, and headed out into the crap, puddles splashing around me as I drove.

I stopped the Jeep in front of Carolina's house. Through the rain, I could see a light on in the living room. I turned off the engine, threw open the Jeep door, and dashed up to the front door and knocked. I looked like I'd jumped in the shower with my clothes on.

Carolina opened the door. "Noah? What are you doing out?" She stepped out of the way and motioned for me to come in.

I came into the entryway, water snaking off me onto her floor.

"Hold on," Carolina said. "I'll get a towel."

She came back and handed me a yellow bath towel. I wiped my face. It smelled like the laundry detergent I remembered her using as a kid, but I couldn't place the name.

I dried off my hair and rubbed the towel over my arms before handing it back to her. "Thanks."

"You're welcome. Why are you out in this?"

"I just got back from San Francisco."

Apprehension trickled onto her face. "Oh." She pointed toward the sofa. "Sit down."

"Simington told me a little more this time," I said, falling onto the couch.

She sat down next to me. "Is that right?" She was trying to mask her anxiety, but it seeped into her words. I couldn't blame her.

"I know you said before that you only heard from him twice after you told him to get lost," I said. "Did he ever mention the name Landon Keene?"

She thought hard for a moment, then shook her head. "Not that I recall. Our conversations were brief. The second time was a little longer I guess, but it was because I was reluctant to give him your address." She shook her head again. "No. He didn't mention that name. Why?"

I hadn't decided yet what to tell her about Keene. But it didn't seem like I had any choice other than to tell her exactly who he was.

"Simington worked for him," I told her. "And he claims that he killed the two men in El Centro because Keene threatened us."

"Us?"

"You and me."

She tilted her head, curious. "I'm not sure I understand."

I repeated Simington's story, not getting to the current threats Keene was throwing around.

Carolina shrugged when I finished. "I believe it. The people he hung around with—I'm sure they were capable of making threats like that." She paused. "And carrying them out."

"But do you think that would've been enough for Simington to carry out the murders?" I asked. "Threats to us?"

She leaned back into the sofa and folded her hands in her lap. "You mean, would he have cared enough about you and me to go to jail?"

I nodded because that was exactly what I was asking. The more I thought about Simington's story, the more I got hung up on thinking that protecting Carolina and me was enough justification for committing murder. Maybe he'd sent some money. Maybe he'd kept track of us. But I wasn't certain that meant he cared about our well-being if it meant putting his in jeopardy.

"Honestly, I don't know," she said. "I'm inclined to say yes, though. As many bad things as he was, there was some good, too. When he called me the second time, to find out where you lived . . . he was like the man I met in the bar."

"Which was?"

"Sincere, kind. Almost apologetic for who he was, like he knew he couldn't help it." She looked down at her hands. "I'm not a great judge of character, but I don't think he was playing me that day." She looked back to me. "He truly wanted to know where you were, to see what his son looked like. That's why I gave in and told him." She shifted on the old sofa cushions. "And I think he has always cared for me. He just couldn't do it the way I needed him to."

FORTY-ONE

We sat quiet for a few minutes, listening to the water tap against the roof and windows.

"I need to tell you something else, then," I finally said.

"You certainly know how to light up a room," she said, raising an eyebrow and smiling.

I appreciated her attempt at humor. The more time I spent with her when she was sober, the more I started to forget about our past and focus on how much I enjoyed being around her.

"I'm like a beacon of sunshine," I said.

She laughed quietly. "Always." She held up a hand. "I'm sorry. I don't mean to interrupt. Something else, you said."

"I seem to have stirred Keene back to life," I said.

"Which means what?"

"Which means I think we need to be careful."

The humor was gone from her expression now. "Why?"

"Because he told me that. Personally."

"You've spoken to this man?"

I recounted what Simington told me and my encounter with Keene at the airport.

"I don't think he's kidding," I said. "He doesn't seem like the type. He killed the lawyer. There's no reason to think he won't kill again if he feels it's necessary. He was at the airport to show me how close he can get to me."

She wrapped her arms around herself like she was cold. "A beacon of sunshine."

"I'm sorry," I told her. "But I felt like I needed to tell you."

She nodded. "No, no. It's not your fault. I was teasing you, and it was inappropriate." She put her hands on her knees. "What are you going to do?"

"I'm not sure yet. I need to think some things over."

Her eyes zeroed in on me. "Don't let him go because of me, Noah. I'll be alright."

I didn't respond.

"If he killed that lawyer and he's partly responsible for Russell's situation, you should do what you can to make him pay," she said. "Do not back away from this because of me. If you have other reasons, that's fine. But don't do it on my behalf." She reached out and touched my arm. "I can take care of myself."

I wasn't sure that she could, but I appreciated what she was saying. Something else was nagging at me, though.

"Would he lie to me?" I asked. "Simington?"

A rumble of thunder echoed outside, the rain still slapping against the windows.

"Probably," Carolina said. "I'd like to think that, with where he is now, with not much time left, he wouldn't. At least to you. But that might be wishing for too much."

That was what had been running through my thoughts since leaving the prison. What if he was trying to manipulate me? To get me to do something he wanted done? What if the facts weren't as he presented them? What if he knew by pushing me in the right direction, I'd go after Keene? Was there something in it for him?

"I just can't help but think he's doing this for some other reason," I said.

"Doing what?"

"Talking to me. Telling me these things about what happened and about Keene. Is there something in it for him?" I looked at her. "Why does he give me Keene's name to begin with if he knows that Keene is a threat?"

She squeezed my arm. "I don't know. With Russell, I could never tell."

"I mean, he gives me Keene's name. He knows I'll look him up. Why give it to me at all and then tell me to stay away from him after I found him?"

"It may be just like he said. Maybe he was hoping that this man would be dead and gone. Maybe he wanted to know that, to give him some peace before his own death. I'm not saying he's incapable of telling the truth, Noah. What he's told you may be exactly as it is."

I knew she was right. I would have to make my own decision based on what I wanted to do. No one else was going to give me a reason. I needed to own the decision. That didn't make it any easier, though.

"Noah?" Carolina said.

"Yeah?"

Her fingers pressed into my skin. "It's okay to be upset about this."

"I know," I said.

"Do you? It doesn't seem like it."

I turned away, watching the rain slide down the glass. Again, Carolina had surprised me with her ability to read me.

"I don't want to care if he dies," I said. "I really don't. I know that if he lived, we wouldn't have a relationship." I hesitated. "But it's like . . . it's like I want to just know he's around. So I can be pissed off at him. I don't think I can be angry at him after he's dead." I turned back to Carolina. "Dumb, huh?"

She slid her hand to mine and forced her fingers into mine. She covered our hands with her other. "No, it's not dumb. It's exactly right."

We sat there, listening to the thunder and the rain, thinking about that.

FORTY-TWO

I left Carolina's and spent a couple hours busying myself with errands—groceries, gas, mail. But nothing cleared my head and I eventually found myself pointed in the direction of Coronado. I wanted to see Liz. After seeing Simington so isolated, I didn't want to be alone, not even for a night.

The rain was splashing off the bridge, billowing into the bay like small explosions as I crossed over to the island. The normally bright lights of downtown were muted and murky.

I ran up the path to Liz's house, and she opened before I could knock, waving me in from out of the tropical weather. She handed me a towel.

"I was wondering when I was going to hear from you," she said.

I wiped off my face, dropped the towel, and pulled her to me, kissing her. Her hands were on my chest at first, protesting being pushed up against a soaking wet human being, but then her hands slipped around my neck and she forgot about my wet condition.

When I finally let her go, she stepped back and put her hand to her chest. "Wow. Nice to see you."

I smiled. "You, too."

"What brought that on?"

"Seeing you."

"Ah."

"I'd like to see more of you. Right now."

She reached out for my hand, an electric charge between us that I'd never felt.

"This way," she said, pulling me toward the bedroom.

Our clothes were off before we made it to the bed, and our bodies clung together like magnets. All of the anger and sadness that had permeated my existence for the last few hours dissipated as I lost myself in Liz, the one person I knew for certain wanted nothing from me other than for me to be who I was. And as we moved together, everything feeling right and simple, all I wanted was to love her.

When we'd finished, we lay there in the dark, the rain moving down her window in silver streams. Her head was on my chest, and her breathing was in rhythm with mine. I put my face into her hair, taking in the scent of coconut, mint, and sweat. I kissed the top of her head.

She rolled over so her head was on my shoulder and she could see me. "Don't take this the wrong way, but was there something in the water in San Francisco?"

"Not that I know of."

"Because if there is, we should bottle it and start selling it. Sales will dwarf every other sex drug on the market, and we'll be able to bathe in the money."

I laughed and rubbed her back. "I just missed you."

She wrapped an arm around my chest. "I missed you, too."

The rain tapped against the window like it wanted in.

"How'd it go?" she asked.

"It went."

"That bad?"

"I don't know, Liz," I said, sighing. "I don't know if was bad or good or something else."

"You wanna tell me?"

I didn't want to talk about it, but I wanted to tell her because if anyone could make sense of it, Liz could. I trusted her.

I told her about my conversation with Simington and then meeting up with Keene in the airport. None of it sounded any different than when I'd spilled it all to Carolina.

Her arm tightened around my chest when I'd finished. "Rough," she said. "I'm sorry."

I nodded awkwardly, my head sunk into the pillow.

"Simington didn't know about Darcy's death?"

"If he did, he didn't show it."

"You believe what he said about Keene?"

"I guess. I don't think I can know for sure, though," I said. "He could be maneuvering me, but so far what he's said seems to be true." I pressed my hand into the small of her back, feeling the heat of her skin up against me. "Keene's a bad guy. That's one thing I'm positive of."

She threw her leg over mine beneath the sheets. The rain was tossing awkward shadows into the room, and I stared over Liz at the window. The moon was obscured by a thick rain cloud.

"Simington was definite about not getting another attorney?" Liz asked.

"Yep."

She put her hand on my cheek and moved my face down so I could see her.

"I'm sorry," she said.

I nodded without saying anything. I tried to look away, but she held my face in place.

"I'm sorry that you're having to deal with all of this," she said, the intensity in her eyes clear even in the dark. "But it doesn't change who you are."

"I know that, Liz," I said. "I do. I'm past that."

"So where are you, then?"

I traced her spine with my fingers. "Trying to figure out what to do next. If anything."

She shivered against me. "If anything?"

"Why am I doing this?" I said. "Simington's going to die no matter what I do. Darcy's dead, and I'm not going to change that. Keene deserves to go to jail—or worse— but I'm not sure it's my place to see that that happens. If digging any more into what happened puts Carolina or me in jeopardy, I don't see the justification. So why not just let it go?"

"Do you feel responsible for Darcy?"

"No, I don't think so," I said. "I really don't. She came to me. She had to know what she was getting in the middle of. I'm not saying that makes what happened to her any less wrong, but I don't feel like it was on my watch."

"I talked to Klimes this morning," she said. "They still don't really have anything."

"I'm not surprised. It feels to me like Keene knows what he's doing. He wouldn't have left any tracks."

"You're certain it was him?"

"Yeah."

A gust of wind blew against the house, a surge of rain hitting harder and louder with a sound like someone had overturned a bucket of water on the roof.

"You asked why you were doing this," she said.

"Right. I'm not sure why."

She propped her head up on her hand, her elbow buried in the pillow. She pushed her hair away from her face, so it fell over to the side, covering her arm. "I think I know why."

I rolled on my side and matched her pose, putting my head on my hand. "Tell me."

"You sure?"

"Your opinion matters more than the rest combined."

She smiled, her long eyelashes fluttering in the dark. "Because it's right. And it's a way of helping him. Your father."

I had blanched every other time someone had called Simington that. But Liz wasn't saying it to make a point. She was merely stating the truth, and it was time for me to start letting that go.

"How?" I asked.

"You can't save him from execution," she explained. "But you can make sure he doesn't die solely responsible for the murders of those men. You can let the world know Simington wasn't the only bad guy involved."

"Is that worth it?" I said. "People will think what they want to think."

She placed a finger on my chest. "It will change the way you think. You'll know that even if Simington wasn't who you wanted him to be, at least it wasn't all on him. He told you this was going to be the one good thing he does." She leaned closer. "Maybe it's up to you to see that that's what happens. That the one good thing Simington ends up being responsible for is the arrest and punishment of Keene." She paused. "And maybe that will let you remember him in another way than the way you think about him now."

I put my hand on the finger she had in the center of my chest. I pulled it to my lips, and kissed her fingernail.

"I'm not sure if you're right," I said. "But thank you."

"For what?"

"You're giving me permission to keep going on this," I said. "You don't even know if you're right, but it's your way of telling me not to give up."

She slid closer to me, the mint from her hair washing over me again. "Just do what you have to do. Do what's right."

I pulled her close and kissed her. I tilted my forehead against hers. "I love you."

She pushed me onto my back and slid on top of me, a here-comes-trouble grin flashing through the darkness. "Prove it."

FORTY-THREE

Thick gray clouds hung outside Liz's window when I woke the next morning. The rain had stopped overnight but seemed ready to empty out of the low sky at any moment.

I untangled myself from Liz and the blankets, put on my jeans and a T-shirt, and headed to the kitchen. I started the coffee for Liz, poured some cereal in a bowl, and sat in her living room, eating and watching the puffy clouds drift along the harbor, obscuring the buildings on the other side.

Halfway into a second bowl, I knew Liz was right. The reason I was keeping my teeth in this was so maybe I could change the way I thought about Russell Simington in future years. It was probably misguided thinking on my part, but I didn't have much else. Never having known my father had allowed me to put my feelings in a nice, tidy little box—I hated him. But, now, having met him, even knowing who he was and what he'd done in his life, a microscopic part of me wanted desperately to find something good. If I could bring down Keene, it would give me something.

Liz stumbled into the living room wearing gray sweats and a blue long-sleeve T-shirt. She was hugging her mug of coffee like it might try to escape as she collapsed onto the sofa next to me. Definitely not a morning person.

She finished the coffee and said, "It's gross out."

"I'd say."

"Not supposed to rain like this here. Isn't that why we tolerate the traffic and earthquakes?"

"You'd think."

She grunted, walked back into the kitchen, and returned with a newly filled cup. She sat down again and looked at me. "Morning."

"Good morning."

"Think I forgot to say that the first time I came out."

"Well, it's gross out, and you were focused on that."

She sipped from the mug, nodding.

"Plans for today?" I asked.

"Meeting at ten," she said, grimacing at either the idea of the meeting or having to leave the house in crappy weather. "Then I'll wait for the bad guys to call me." She looked at me. "You?"

"I'll go home and see if Carter and Miranda dug anything up while I was gone. Then I'm not sure."

"I'll talk to Klimes again," she said. "See if he knows anything more."

"Tell Zanella I said hello, too. I miss him."

"Grow up. What did he say to you anyway?"

"You don't wanna know."

"Actually, I do. That's why I asked."

"Forget it," I said, sorry I'd brought it up.

"Let me guess," she said, holding a finger to her chin like she was thinking hard. "Something about you and me? Maybe something sexual? Something insulting? I'm sure I've *never* heard anything like that before."

Liz took a lot of crap for being a woman in a job that was traditionally reserved for old-school men. She liked to act like it didn't bother her, but I knew the barbs sometimes got through.

"You got the gist of it," I said.

She shook her head, staring into her coffee. "Zanella's not the brightest guy. Figured he was working with a limited repertoire of derogatory remarks. Next time, let it go."

"Next time, I'll break his jaw."

"No, you won't," she said, moving her eyes from the coffee to me. "I don't need you defending me. I appreciate it, but I don't need it. Especially not with a guy like that. I can handle him fine on my own."

I nodded, but I knew if he popped off again, I'd hit him again. Testosterone isn't rational.

"I need to get in the shower and get moving," she said, sighing, glancing at the window.

"Me, too."

I found my shoes and sweatshirt, wishing we could just spend the day like we'd spent the night. But I didn't know if that was because I wanted to stay or because I wanted to avoid the problems I needed to go solve.

Liz met me at the front door. "Call me later and let me know what's going on."

"I will."

"And be careful," she said, her eyes warning me not to do anything stupid. "If you need help, ask for it."

I put my arms around her waist and pulled her to me. "I will."

"You won't, but I thought I should say it anyway," she said.

I leaned down and kissed her.

"I will," I whispered. "I promise. I won't let you down."

She held my face in her hands. "Don't worry about letting me down. Just do what you need to do."

FORTY-FOUR

When it rains in Southern California, we drive as though we've never seen rain before. We go about ten miles an hour, jam on the brakes at every opportunity, and try to rearend as many other cars as possible.

That's why the normally twenty minute drive back to Mission Beach took me over an hour on the wet freeway.

I walked up the boardwalk to my house. Storms had a way of wreaking havoc on most everything else, but they stirred up the ocean in a good way. The swells rose up with a little more intensity than on sunny days, their usually unspectacular waves coming in higher and heavier, crashing with an attitude.

I was thinking about pulling my full wetsuit from the closet when I walked into my place and found Miranda straddling Carter on the living room floor, his arms pinned above his head and his eyes full of fear.

"I told you you'd go down like a rag doll," she said to him.

Carter's eyes shifted to me. "Help."

Miranda turned around. "He bet me I couldn't throw him to the floor."

"Good bet," I said.

Miranda slid off him, and he jumped to his feet like nothing had happened.

"Lucky," he said.

Miranda grunted and pushed some of the black hair away from her face. "How'd it go?"

"Awesome," I replied, making a face. "You two learn anything?"

"I learned Magilla Gorilla isn't that tough," she said, glancing at Carter.

Carter looked like a child whose favorite toy had been taken from him by a bully. "Whatever." He looked at me. "It was Keene who was down here."

"Positive?" I asked, unsurprised.

"Pretty positive," he said. "We talked to about thirty people. Houses on the walk and a couple in the alleys. We got several descriptions that match the guy."

"The night before Darcy was found?"

Miranda nodded. "Yeah, and one guy who swears he saw him two days before."

I looked at Carter. "Who?"

"Dude up on Cohassett. Said he saw him at Roberto's and on the beach."

"Believable?"

"Complete stoner, but he seemed somewhat lucid when we talked to him."

Two days prior. Which meant Keene had been keeping tabs on me. Again, not a surprise, but not something I was thrilled to hear either.

Miranda looked at Carter. "You owe me a meal."

Carter grimaced. "I know."

"I want it. Now."

"So order a pizza. It's almost lunchtime. I'll pay."

She shook her head. "Not a chance." She turned to me. "Where's an expensive place down here?"

"Lamont Street Grill is good," I said.

Carter gave me the finger.

Miranda turned back to him. "That's where we're going."

"Have fun," I said, walking into the kitchen.

"You're not coming?" Carter asked, both curious and hopeful.

"Don't want to ruin your date," I said. "And I'm not in the mood."

"Why not?" Miranda asked.

There were a lot of reasons, but I didn't feel the need to get into them at that moment. I needed to clear my head.

"I'm tired," I said. "Go. I'll fill you guys in later."

"On what?" Carter asked.

I didn't answer because I wasn't sure.

FORTY-FIVE

Call it maturity. Call it good decision making. Call it whatever you want, but I'd come to the decision that no matter how badly I wanted Keene myself, I wouldn't be able to do much with him. The smart course of action was to talk to Klimes and tell him what I'd learned.

It took a sandwich and two beers before arriving at that conclusion. Keene wasn't going to be phased by any more threats I made. There wasn't any guarantee that Klimes would help me out, but I thought he'd at least be honest with me about whether he could do anything.

Dispatch patched me through to his cell. "Klimes."

"Klimes, it's Noah Braddock. Am I catching you at a bad time?"

I heard paper crumple through the line. "Nope. Just finishing a shitty lunch. What's up?"

"Remember that name I asked you to check? Keene?"

"Sure."

"He's your guy."

"On the dead girl?"

"Yeah."

"Tell me."

I started with what Simington told me at the prison, including Keene and the smuggling, and ended with Carter and Miranda's door-to-door.

"We didn't get anybody to give those IDs when we asked," Klimes said, annoyed.

"What can I tell you? Tight-knit group down here. They know Carter. They don't know you. And Zanella's an asshole."

He chuckled. "I suppose. Gonna need to talk to those folks your friends talked to, though."

"Okay. I'll make it work."

"And I had Keene on my short list."

"How's that?"

"Son, you asked me to run a name and then gave me a bullshit story about it. I may be fat and ugly, but I'm not dumb. I did my own, more extensive check. I tied some loose ends together with him and Simington."

"You talk to him?"

"Not yet. Elusive little fella."

"You have an address?"

"A bad one. And if I had a good one, I wouldn't give it to you. You're a bit too close to all this, Noah."

He was right. Having Keene's address would probably be too much temptation for me.

"That's fine. I just wanted you to know."

"Thanks. Get me the names of your neighbors. ASAP."

I told him I would and hung up.

A cannon of thunder boomed outside. The thrashing ocean looked like a giant bathtub beneath the storm. It should have been a great time to hit the water.

Stupid rain.

FORTY-SIX

Ringing.

In the distance.

I forced my eyes open. I'd fallen asleep on the sofa.

And the phone was ringing.

I scrambled around in the dark living room and found the phone on the dining room table. "Hello?"

"Well, I decided I'm not the patient type," Landon Keene said.

The fogginess from sleep lifted immediately, and I gripped the phone tighter.

"Kid, you listening?" he said.

"Fuck you."

"Good, good," he said. "Like I said, I'm not good with patience. Decided I couldn't leave it to you to make the right decision. Know what I mean?"

My fingers tingled. "No."

"You seem a little stubborn. Just like your old man. Couldn't risk that you'd do something dumb. Like repeating what he told you."

"You better run, asshole," I said. "I've already told the cops about your operation. They're coming for you. And I hope they have to shoot you to catch you."

"That right?" he asked.

"Yeah, that's right."

"Guess I made the right decision then."

My skin went cold and I couldn't find any words.

The line buzzed. The room lit up for a moment as lightning struck in the distance. He knew he had me.

"The look in her eyes," he said, a soft laugh drifting through the phone. "She was so surprised to see me."

The room hollowed out. My heart rate accelerated like someone had pushed a button. Spots started flashing between my eyes. I knew I shouldn't have listened to Carolina and left her alone.

"If you—"

"I did. Maybe now you'll get it." He hung up.

FORTY-SEVEN

I dialed Carolina's number twice as I sped from Mission Beach to Bay Park.

No answer.

I called Carter. He answered on the first ring

"Where are you?" I yelled.

"Driving around," he said. "I'm showing—"

"Get to my mother's! Now!"

"Ten minutes," he said and hung up.

I threw the phone at the floor of the Jeep, so angry for listening to her and letting her convince me she could take care of herself. Not taking Keene seriously enough.

I'd fucked up.

The Jeep hydroplaned through the puddles on Morena, spraying water like giant rooster tails. People were honking and flashing their brights at me as I swerved around them.

I slammed on the brakes in front of Carolina's house, sliding nearly twenty feet before coming to a crooked stop. Carter's Ram Charger did the same on the opposite side of the street.

"What happened?" Carter yelled through the rain.

"Tell her to stay in the car," I yelled back, gesturing at Miranda as I drew my gun.

He yelled something to her and produced his own gun.

I sprinted up the walk and saw a light on through the front window. I felt Carter right on my heels.

I hit the front door with my shoulder at full speed, and it collapsed like cardboard. I went down with it and somersaulted into the living room.

There was a clatter in the kitchen, and when I looked up, Carolina was aiming her own gun at us.

FORTY-EIGHT

"Noah?" Carolina said, lowering the gun and looking at us like we'd lost our minds. "Carter? What are you doing?"

I got to my feet, the blood pulsing in my ears, and scanned the room. Everything looked fine.

"I'm not sure, Ms. B.," Carter said, his gun still up. "Noah told me to meet him here. I followed him in."

I kept my gun level, moving it back and forth. "You didn't answer your phone."

"I ran to the store," she said, bewildered. "Noah, what is going on?"

I moved into the back of the house and checked the other rooms. Was Keene screwing with me?

"He wasn't here?" I asked when I came back out.

"Who?" Carolina asked, still looking at me like I was crazy.

"Keene."

She blinked several times. "No. I was home all day. I ran to the store to get eggs. I haven't seen him."

"Did he call you?" I said, hearing the frustration in my voice.

"No. There was nothing on the machine."

Keene had made a point of mentioning Carolina at the airport. He wanted me to know he was watching me.

She was so surprised to see me.

Keene didn't strike me as the type to tease.

"Noah," Carter said. "What's going on? You're freaking us out."

The room hollowed out again. My stomach dropped.

Keene wasn't the type to tease.

You should've seen her.

He knew every move I was making. Every place I'd been. Every person I'd talked to.

He'd used Carolina's name. He hadn't used Liz's.

But he knew.

FORTY-NINE

"Wellton!" I screamed into the phone as Carter and I flew down the freeway in his car. We'd left Miranda with my mother. "Tell me you know where she is."

I'd called her home and her cell and the station. She was nowhere to be found. Wellton was my last shot.

"Braddock?" he said, confused. "What the hell—"

"Liz! Is she with you?"

"No, man. Haven't seen her since this afternoon. She said—"

"Get someone to her house! Now!"

"What's going on?" he said, his tone sharper now, on alert.

"Just do it! Please."

"I'm on it," he said and clicked off.

I clutched the phone, feeling like it could shatter against the bones in my hand.

"Come on, come on," I said, rocking back and forth in the passenger seat.

We were halfway over the bridge now, and Carter was doing ninety.

"She can handle herself, Noah," he said, laying on the horn as we came up on the bumper of a truck. The truck moved over quickly, and Carter accelerated. "She's a cop."

"Why didn't she answer?" I asked. "Why? Fuck!"

We came to the bottom of the bridge, and he swung the huge car to the right, the rear fishtailing behind us.

"Your mom was at the store," he said, not sounding confident. "Maybe she's out."

His argument was rational. She could have been out anywhere without her phone. A five-minute trip to the store or the beach.

But it didn't feel right.

He hit the brakes, and I was out of the car before it stopped in front of her place, tumbling to the wet street, the rain stinging my face. I jumped up and ran to the house.

No lights.

I hit her door the same way I'd hit Carolina's and pain radiated through my shoulder. Liz's much heavier door fought me a little more, but landed on the floor with a thud, and I stumbled in on top of it.

I stood still for a moment. The room was black and quiet. All I could hear was Carter's and my breathing and the rain spanking the pavement outside.

"Liz?" I yelled.

Nothing.

"I got upstairs," Carter said, moving past me, his gun up and ready. "You get the kitchen?"

I took a deep breath, bent my knees, and stepped quickly from the living room into the kitchen. I rotated my gun through the room. Dishes in the sink. A napkin on the table. Lightning flashed outside the window.

No one.

I stood up and took another deep breath, trying to gain control. Maybe Keene had just played me, messed with my head. Trying to show me he was in control. He'd gotten in my head at the airport. He'd seen it, and now he was seeing what he could do to me.

I walked out of the kitchen and Carter was at the top of the stairs. He took one step down, his entire body lethargic and heavy. When I saw the expression on his face, an expression I'd never seen before—disbelief, confusion—I knew.

FIFTY

She was on the bed and, in the dark, appeared to be sleeping.

I moved closer and felt my gun slip out of my hand and fall to the floor.

Her eyes were open and her arms outstretched, like she'd been reaching for something. A deep, red circle on her chest half a foot in diameter had stained the T-shirt she was wearing and bled into the sheet.

I sat down on the edge of the bed and touched her hand. It was still warm, and I laced my fingers with hers, squeezing hard, as though I could transfer my life to hers.

But I knew that I couldn't.

I heard sirens in the distance and shouts downstairs, but they seemed further away.

I reached out and covered her eyes, gently pushing her lids down.

The tears fell off my face onto hers, and in the murky, rainy moonlight, it looked like it was Liz who was crying rather than me.

FIFTY-ONE

Commotion.

People were coming and going. Carter sat next to me on the sofa in Liz's living room. I was vaguely aware of all this, yet completely removed from it. I wasn't numb; I could feel a dull pain in my stomach that pulsed with each breath. It was more like I was trying to wake up and couldn't clear my head.

Wellton was standing in front of me. "Did you hear me?"

I looked up. "What?"

His eyes were blazing in the dark room. "I asked when you last spoke to her."

"Oh. I . . . um . . . this morning. I was here. Then I left."

"Where'd you go?" he asked.

I'd walked out of the house. Told her I'd do the right thing. That I wouldn't let her down.

"Where did you go?" Wellton repeated, his voice seared with anger.

"I . . . home, I guess."

"You guess?"

"Easy," Carter said.

Wellton pointed at Carter. "Shut the hell up. My partner is dead, and I want to know why."

Carter stood and started yelling at him, but his words faded in the air.

I'd told her I wouldn't let her down.

But I had.

Why had I even left her?

Why hadn't I seen it?

The ache in my stomach pulsed like a strobe. My arms and legs felt light, like they were attached but I couldn't control them.

Two officers grabbed Carter and pulled him away from Wellton, and the words in the room exploded back into my head.

"Leave him alone!" Carter was yelling. "He found her! How do you *think* he feels?"

"She was my partner!" Wellton was screaming back, his hands now on Carter's shirt.

"And she was more to him!" Carter yelled back, straining against the grasp of the two officers.

I knew they were talking about me, but I couldn't engage.

I felt Liz's hands on my face. We were standing in her doorway. Her eyes were right in front of me. I could smell her hair, her skin, feel her breath against my skin, her lips against mine.

Don't worry about letting me down. Just do what you need to do.

I'd let her down.

I hadn't done what I needed to do.

And now she was gone.

FIFTY-TWO

I don't know how long we stayed at Liz's. I know that I tried to answer more of Wellton's questions. I know that he and Carter continued to yell at each other. I know that Klimes and Zanella showed up at some point. And I know I saw her body come down on a stretcher beneath a white sheet.

That, for sure, I know.

At some point, Carter took me home. The rain was still pounding against the streets and his car as we drove.

"We'll find him," Carter said.

I didn't know who he meant, and I didn't ask. My mouth was sealed shut, like someone had filled it with cement. My eyes stung. Something throbbed in my ears.

Carter was talking, but I was only hearing bits and pieces.

". . . I don't know where . . ."

A chill rattled my body. I looked across the bay as we neared Mission Beach and saw Liz standing in the water.

". . . and no one will . . ."

I closed my eyes, trying to abate the stinging.

". . . don't let it . . ."

I leaned my head against the glass, the cold window sticking against my cheek. The car was spinning.

I felt Carter's hand on my shoulder. "Hey. Are you alright?"

My head fell forward in something resembling a nod.

I closed my eyes again, and when I opened them we were in the alley next to my place. I shoved the door open and slid out, my legs feeling awkward and stiff beneath me. I looked up, letting the rain pelt my face.

Carter appeared next to me and held out a hand to help steady me.

I waved him off and forced myself to walk toward the house. I got the door open. It was pitch black inside. I heard Carter come in behind me.

I didn't stop until I found my bed. I collapsed into it, shut my eyes, and wished for nothing else than to never wake up.

FIFTY-THREE

Flashbulbs kept going off in my head, showing me snapshots I didn't know I'd taken.

Liz and me in high school, talking in the hallway. She was a year older than me. She was telling me she wanted to interview me for the paper. I said okay.

Then she was yelling at me. We were in a parking lot. She was furious with me, and I was yelling back at her.

We were in her office. She was pointing a finger at me.

We were sitting on her deck, drinking beer. I could see her legs in the dark.

I was driving the Jeep. Liz was sitting next to me. We were on the 101, the sun setting to our left.

We were in her bed. She was on top of me, sweating, our eyes locked as we moved together.

Then we were in the ocean. I was yelling something across the water to her. My voice was coming out of my mouth, but I couldn't make out what I was saying. She was coming toward me, the water splashing around her legs as she got closer.

I was still talking, but I couldn't hear the words.

And then she was gone, and I was standing in the ocean by myself, still saying whatever I'd been saying, turning around in circles, looking for her.

FIFTY-FOUR

My eyes opened, and the daylight forced me to squeeze them shut again.

I opened them more carefully this time. Muted sunlight filtered into the room. The sheets on my bed were twisted around me like ribbons, and I struggled to pull myself out of them. I pushed up and sat on the edge of the mattress. My head ached, and it felt like an entire cotton field had grown inside my mouth. I stood and walked out to the living room.

Carter was on the sofa, watching the television with the sound turned down.

He turned around. "Hey." He reached over, grabbed the remote, and shut off the TV.

I opened the fridge, found a bottle of water, and downed it in about four swallows.

"You alright?" he asked.

I threw the empty bottle in the sink. "Time is it?" My throat was tight and raw.

"About four o'clock."

I looked out the window. The weak sunlight I'd seen in my room was about to disappear again behind clouds the color of steel.

"You spend the night here?" I asked.

He hesitated. "Both nights."

I looked at him. "Both?"

"You haven't come out of your room for almost two days, man."

I nodded like I knew that. I grabbed another bottle of water out of the fridge and drank half of it. "Where's Miranda?"

"My place."

The clouds swallowed the sun, and the rain started to fall.

"Still raining?" I said.

"It's barely stopped," he said. "Wellton wants you—"

"Don't."

He nodded slowly. "Okay."

"Not yet," I said, watching the waves tumble outside.

Neither of us said anything for a few minutes. I watched the water, and he watched me.

"There's one thing, Noah," he finally said. "I think you should know."

I emptied the bottle, tossed it into the sink with the other, and took a deep breath. "What?"

"Tomorrow. Ten AM," he said, his voice cracking a little. "Her funeral."

I grabbed another bottle of water from the fridge and went back to my room.

WEEK THREE

FIFTY-FIVE

Police funerals are like parades.

Everyone gets dressed up. There is marching, speeches, and music. The dead are treated like heroes, as they should be.

I assume they did the same for Liz, but I didn't go to watch it.

Carter and I—several times I'd told him I was fine, that he could leave me alone, but he never bought it and he was probably correct not to—waited for the pomp and circumstance to end and then drove out to the cemetery on Coronado. He dropped me off at the gate and said he'd be back in an hour.

I wandered through the park, headstones rising out of the muddy ground like dominoes, until I found the one I was looking for.

Elizabeth Shannon Santangelo.

I knelt down next to the freshly turned earth and ran my hand across the dirt, knowing she was somewhere beneath it.

I wasn't sure what I believed when it came to the afterlife. Like most people, I hoped that there was something else, that in some way we lived on after our lives were extinguished here. But maybe that was just a concept, developed and perpetuated throughout time, meant to help us deal with the finality of death.

As I let the dirt fall through my fingers, I chose to believe that there was something else, because believing that this was the final stop for Liz was too much for me to bear.

The wind picked up and whistled across the cemetery, the rain taking a momentary respite.

I'd heard people say that when someone you care about dies unexpectedly, it doesn't seem real.

That wasn't the experience I was having.

Sitting in a cemetery, next to a headstone with her name engraved in elegant letters, made it very real.

I was surprised to see the headstone already in place, but the department arranged her funeral and I assumed that they expedited the creation and placement of the marker, not wanting one of their own to go anonymously into the earth.

I ran my index finger across the letters. The stone was cold, and it sent a chill through my arm, down my spine, and into my heart.

I wasn't there to say goodbye. Maybe I'd be ready to do that another time, but not now.

I just wanted to be near her.

But as I sat there, knowing she wasn't coming back, the chill in my body began to pulse, like someone was tapping my insides with a frozen hammer. Everything hurt.

I stared at her name on that headstone for a long time. There were no tears. I don't know why. But they didn't come. I knew they'd arrive later, at some unexpected and irrelevant point when I finally gave in to being without her.

The wind gathered speed and rain drops smacked the back of my neck.

I grabbed another handful of dirt. I folded my fingers around it and squeezed.

As the rain pelted me, I stood. I opened my hand, and it looked to me like some of the dirt had disappeared. It had probably just slipped out of my hand, but I liked the idea that it had forced its way into my skin, into my veins, and into my soul to stay with me forever.

I looked down at the earth, the rain matting it down like it was trying to put a protective seal over her.

"I'm sorry I let you down," I told her, my voice cracking, as I backed away from Liz Santangelo's grave. "But I will fix it."

FIFTY-SIX

"What are we going to do?" Carter asked.

We were headed back to Mission Beach, a light rain slicking the highway.

"Moffitt first," I said. "After I talk to him, I'll have a better idea of what I want to do."

"Miranda's getting restless," Carter said, swinging his car onto Mission Bay Drive. "She feels like Darcy's getting forgotten in all of this—"

"I don't care. Tell her to go home. Or don't. But I don't care what she does." The gray clouds were sinking lower, obscuring even the rooftops of the hotels as we moved over Bahia Point. "I'm off Darcy's case. The police can worry about her. It's not my concern."

"She still thinks you're working to help Simington," he said.

I laughed, but it sounded harsh and bitter. "She's wrong. I'm done with him."

Carter pulled to a stop behind my place in the alley. Klimes' Crown Victoria was a block up, but I didn't mention it.

"Okay," he said. "I'll get it settled with her and wait to hear from you. Then we get it done."

I opened the door and stepped out of the car. "Right. I'll call you."

He sped off down the alley.

He kept saying "we," and I knew he meant it. I knew he'd do anything—no matter the consequence—to help me.

But there wasn't going to be any *we* in getting this thing done.

Keene had taken Liz from me.

And now I was going to take Keene from everyone else.

FIFTY-SEVEN

I walked into my living room and saw Klimes, Zanella, and Wellton standing outside on my patio, each holding an umbrella. Klimes was peering in the door and raised an eyebrow when he saw me.

I opened the slider and let them in.

"Didn't see you today," Klimes said, closing his umbrella and dropping it on the patio. "Wanted to make sure you were fine."

Zanella and Wellton came in behind him.

"I'm fine," I said.

"This always sounds empty," Klimes said, running a hand across his jaw. "But I'm really sorry, Noah. Not just for you, but for us, too. She was a good cop."

I nodded but said nothing. Zanella looked uncomfortable, refusing to meet my eyes. Wellton looked exhausted, his eyes rimmed with red, his tie pulled loose at the neck.

"We're looking for Keene now," Klimes said. "Have you heard from him?"

"No."

Klimes nodded, like that's what he expected. "Okay. Alright."

"Why are you here?" I asked.

Klimes bit his lip and glanced at the other two. Zanella still looked nervous, and Wellton's eyes just seemed vacant.

"We wanted to check on you. We know how hard this must be," Klimes said.

"I'm fine. But you're lying," I said. "Why are you here?"

"We want to make sure you don't do anything stupid," Zanella blurted out.

"Like what? Hit you again?"

Color rose in Zanella's cheeks.

"I'm ready to go anytime," I said. "Say the word."

I felt drunk. The exhaustion and emotion had pulverized me. I knew that if Zanella made even a minute move in my direction, I would shred him. I was saying stupid things and acting even more stupid. But I didn't care.

"Noah," Klimes said, his voice a little more official now. "We know what you're going through. It'd be natural for you to wanna go get Keene. Hell, you've got an entire department that wants him now. But we need to make sure it goes down the right way."

"Really? And what's the right way?"

"You know what that is, Noah," Klimes said, trying to soothe me. "Let us do our work and bring him in the right way."

I shook my head, the bitter laugh coming out again. "Right."

"Think about it," Klimes said. "We find Keene's body, you know who the first person is we have to come to? You. We don't want that. We'll get him. And trust me. Nothing a bunch of cops like more than bringing in some piece of shit who killed one of our own."

"How about you, Zanella?" I said, turning sharply to him. "You feel that way too? I mean, before, you told me that Santangelo didn't mean shit to you. I believe because she was fucking me."

That wasn't exactly what he'd said, but I wasn't thinking exactly straight.

Zanella flushed again, started to speak, then stopped. He cleared his throat. "She was a cop. He killed her. That's all I care about."

I wanted to fight with someone, but even Zanella could see it and wouldn't take the bait.

"She wouldn't want it that way, Noah," Klimes said. "We both know it. She would not want you to take the fall on this."

I took a step closer to Klimes. "Do not tell me what she would've wanted. Ever."

"We're your friends, Noah," Klimes said. "We're all on the same side. Let's make sure it stays that way."

He turned to leave, and Zanella quickly followed him out. Wellton lingered in the living room, staring at his shoes.

"Your ride's leaving," I said.

Wellton turned and watched Klimes and Zanella disappear off the patio. Then he looked at me.

"You find him, you call me," he said, his voice rough and low. "Any time, any place. Call me. Not them."

He walked out into the rain.

FIFTY-EIGHT

A knock on the door the next morning startled me out of bed. I grabbed my gun for no other reason than I was hoping it was Landon Keene. I looked through the peephole and saw Miranda.

I opened the door, and she looked at the gun.

"Easy, Homeland Security," she said.

"What do you want?"

"My stuff. I left some of it here."

I stepped aside and let her in, closing the door behind her.

"I'm going home to San Francisco," she said, sitting down on the arm of the sofa.

"Oh. I think your backpack is in the bedroom."

"Great. I have to get back to school. And there's nothing for me to do here anyway," she said, disgust in her voice. "Not like anyone's gonna do anything for Darcy now."

I leaned against the door.

She folded her arms across her chest. "Look, I know your girlfriend is dead. I'm sorry. I really am. But my friend is dead, too. I didn't know your girlfriend, but I did know Darcy. It bothers me that what happened to her is going to take a backseat now."

I understood what Miranda was saying, but it didn't change a thing for me. And I also thought that if I took care of Keene, that would be doing something for Darcy, too. Maybe Miranda didn't see it that way.

"Look, I didn't come here to fight with you," she said. "I came to get my stuff and to confirm that you are off Simington's case."

"Confirmed."

She nodded slowly, not surprised. "Figured as much. I'll see if I can find another attorney to take it over."

"Won't matter. He doesn't want to get off. He's done."

She shrugged her bony shoulders. "Whatever. Darcy would want me to find someone to at least try."

I turned away from her. Trying was a waste of time, and we both knew it. But I didn't doubt she'd go through the motions on Darcy's behalf.

She disappeared into the bedroom and reemerged with her backpack.

"You gonna go see him again?" she asked.

"I don't know."

"If you do, don't go for the wrong reasons."

"And what the hell would those be?"

She clutched the backpack to her body. "I'm guessing you think he might be able to give you some answers, help you solve all this?"

I didn't say anything.

"Then you'll take care of things on your own, right? Exact your own revenge because justice isn't enough?"

I turned and looked at her. "You have a fuckin' point?"

"You hate Simington," she said, tilting her head to the side, like she was trying to get a better look at me. "And, probably, that's fair. He fucked you over, and there's no denying he's a piece of shit." Miranda stepped closer to me. "If you do this, you become him. The whole circle of life thing."

Something resembling an icicle formed in my chest. "Fuck you."

She laughed and smirked at me. "Are you serious? You don't see it? You think because you're hurt, that makes what you're thinking about doing different?"

"You don't know what I'm thinking about doing."

"I don't?" she said, raising the eyebrow with the ring in it. "That vicious scowl you're wearing as a mask? What's that for? That's not grief, Noah. That is hate and anger and I'm-going-to-kill-the-motherfucker-who-did-this-to-me all over your face." She let the eyebrow drop. "And why else would you think about going back to see a man you hate? It's not going to be to tell him you'll miss him."

The icicle grew bigger, and I looked past her to the slider. Rain was slapping the big window, running down the glass in thick, blurred streams, obscuring the ocean.

I moved my gaze back to Miranda. "What about you? You don't want justice for what happened to Darcy? We're talking about one person who did this to both of them."

A moment of hurt passed through her eyes. "Of course I want justice for her. But I want the right kind. Not vigilante shit. Darcy would've hated that. It's exactly what she was fighting against." She shook her head. "I'm angry. I'm hurt. I miss her. But I won't let it ruin my life."

She walked past me to the door and opened it, then paused and turned back to me.

"Killing is killing no matter the reason," Miranda said. "Darcy used to say that a lot because she believed it. I do, too. There's no difference between what Simington did and what you want to do. You can rationalize it all you want, but that won't change it. I can see it in your eyes. You think doing this will make everything right and ruin this guy's life." She threw her backpack over her shoulder. "If you kill him, Noah, the only life it's going to ruin is yours."

FIFTY-NINE

It was two AM, and I wasn't sleeping.

I'd wasted a whole day, pacing my living room, staring out at the black ocean, and ignoring the phone every time it rang. Now I was lying in bed, doing the mental equivalent of pacing.

Second thoughts were invading my head.

Miranda's words had stuck with me. It wasn't that I didn't know that what I wanted to do was dangerous. Or that, in the entire scheme of things, it wouldn't really change anything in my world.

It was anger that was propelling me forward, and I knew that was selfish.

But a man who'd killed two women whom I knew was walking around the streets just like I was. I had a problem with that.

The light shivered through the curtains. I could do the right thing. Let the police do their work and apprehend him. I could report the threats he'd made, tell them about the conversations he and I had. Yes, he was a career criminal and had done a good job, so far, of evading the law. But he'd made a few mistakes in the last few days, and he'd probably be caught. There'd be jail time, then a trial, and then most likely prison.

Then he'd be done walking around.

But I wasn't sure I was alright with that. As long as he was alive, even if he was in prison, I'd be wondering about him, wondering what he was doing, what he was saying. Maybe bragging about Darcy and Liz. And I'd be furious. There wasn't any legal justice that could extinguish that anger.

It would screw up my life, Miranda was right about that. But at the moment, I didn't care. I was lying in bed without Liz, never to feel her hands on my chest, her voice in my ear, or her lips on my cheek again. I didn't feel like anything could screw up my life any further.

I knew that was emotion talking. Everything was still raw. I had no perspective and no distance, two things I knew I needed before making a decision.

I rolled over in the dark and wondered if I'd have the patience to wait for those two things to arrive.

SIXTY

The rain was pounding the beach the next morning, but I decided to go for a run anyway. I needed to get out of my house, even if it meant getting drenched. So for an hour, I ran down the rain-soaked sand, letting the drops of precipitation rip at my face as I went. The exercise didn't do anything for my mood, but my body felt loose and my mind a little sharper.

Carter was on my sofa watching television when I came back.

"Why in God's name would you go running in this shit?" he asked, sitting up and sliding his massive feet off the arm of the sofa.

I peeled off my wet sweatshirt. "Why not? Making yourself at home?"

"You have cable. I don't."

"Right."

I went in the bedroom, stripped out of the rest of my wet clothes and threw on a sweatshirt and jeans. Needing a jolt of caffeine, I grabbed two sodas out of the fridge, handed Carter one, and fell in next to him on the sofa.

"Miranda came to see me yesterday on her way out of town," I said.

"Oh yeah?"

"Yeah. What'd you tell her?"

"Tell her? Nothing."

I stared at him.

He winced, like he knew he'd been caught. "Look. She's not stupid. She sort of figured out what we were talking about doing. She wanted to know. She kind of beat it out of me."

"Beat it out of you?"

"Well, no. But she wouldn't leave me alone until I told her."

I drank from the soda. "You'd be great under torture."

"She'd be great at doing the torture."

I shook my head.

He gulped down the rest of his drink, then looked at me. "What's wrong?"

"Nothing."

"That's a lie in a lot of ways right now for you, Noah," he said, a thin smile on his face. "I'm not looking for a laundry list, but you look . . . preoccupied."

I spun the cold can between my hands, staring at it, but thinking of other things.

"I'm wondering if I'm wrong," I said.

"Wrong?"

"In thinking about . . . doing this."

"You mean taking this motherfucker out?" he asked, almost incredulous.

I drank some more of the soda, then looked at him. "Yeah."

He stared at me for a moment, his eyes surveying me to see if I was serious or if he was missing my point. He leaned forward, resting his elbows on his knees, the soda can dangling from his hand.

"Noah, here's what I know," he said, his voice lower than before, pronouncing each word carefully. "This asshole is partly responsible for your dad being in prison. He killed a woman who came to you for help and dumped her here, in your living room. He's threatened your mother. And he killed Liz." He held the can to his lips then pulled it away. "There is nothing *right* about keeping this guy around."

"I don't disagree with any of that," I said, annoyed that he went for the easy points. "I get all that."

"Then there's nothing else to get," he said, equally annoyed that I was looking at anything other than his points.

"Yeah, there is," I said, concentrating on remaining reasonable. I didn't want to fight with him.

He leaned back in the sofa and held out a hand. "Enlighten me."

"The cops have everything they need to go find him," I said. "Chances are they will."

"Whoopee. Doesn't mean they can arrest him, and even if they do, doesn't mean he'll be convicted." He made a face. "And you think he gives a shit about going to jail? Probably like a vacation home for him."

I could tell he liked countering my arguments.

"Taking Keene out," I said, measuring my words. "It's crossing a line."

"A line that *he's* drawn," Carter said, punching a finger in my direction.

I sighed and sank back into the sofa. Anything I gave him, he was going to find a way to spin it in favor of killing Keene.

"No offense, but it's not like you haven't done it before," he said.

"Different. Way different," I said.

"Really?" he said, raising an eyebrow. "How?"

"Nothing was ever planned out. Nothing was ever premeditated."

"So as long as you don't think about it ahead of time, it's okay?" he deadpanned.

"In a way, yeah. But that's not what I'm saying, and you know it," I said, fidgeting and frowning.

"Then say it, dude," he said. "Say what it really is. What's really holding you back?"

I tilted the can back and finished the soda. I squeezed the aluminum between my hands, the condensation slicking my palms. "I know she would hate it. It's the opposite of everything she believed in. I know that it would disappoint her like nothing else I've ever done. It would make me more like Simington than I want to be. And I could never take that back."

I waited for his response, but he didn't say anything. He stood and walked over to the glass door, one hand in the pocket of his shorts and one clutching the now-crushed soda can.

"I'll buy that more than I'll buy any of your other arguments," he finally said. "I can understand that. But she's gone, and you're here. You'll be the one who has to live with knowing that he's still out there, that no matter what happens to him, he got away with it. And, yeah, to me, even if he's arrested and thrown in a cell, it still seems like he gets away with it. Motherfucker would be a hero in prison for killing a cop."

We were going around in circles, and it wasn't doing me any good.

"And there's one other thing," I said.

He turned away from the glass. "What's that?"

I stood and walked over next to him, my eyes fixated on what looked like a boiling ocean. "No matter what I do, nothing brings her back. Ever." I watched several waves roll in and collapse into a mess of foam. "And I'm not sure anything else matters."

SIXTY-ONE

"I need to get going," Carter said. "Let me know what you decide."

"Do my best not to disappoint you," I said, trying to lighten the mood.

He walked toward the front door and turned around. "You won't disappoint me, Noah. Whatever you end up thinking is right. You have to do what's right for you. You do that, I won't be disappointed."

"Thanks," I said.

He nodded and opened the door.

The alleyway roared and the concussive force of an explosion sent both of us to the floor. I slammed my head against the leg of the dining room table.

I rolled over, gathered my bearings, and sat up. "You alright?"

Carter used the sofa to pull himself up. "What the fuck was that?"

Smoke filled the air and the doorway, but I didn't see any flames. Something was on fire, though. We went out through the slider and around the boardwalk to the alley.

Sirens were already whining in the distance. We turned the corner to the alley.

Carter's truck was a bonfire. Flames shot high into the air, black smoke billowing from beneath what was left. The skull and crossbones on the hood were unrecognizable.

"Was I supposed to be in that?" Carter asked.

Things are gonna start blowing up in your face.

That's what Keene had said.

The first fire engine arrived and filled the alley with red and white lights. The firefighters got to work hooking up a hose, soaking the charred remains of Carter's truck.

Cars didn't just blow up in alleys.

I knew it was Keene.

Maybe he thought he'd scare me off. He'd already figured out that going after the people in my life was more effective than coming directly at me. I hated that he somehow knew that. He was clearly threatened by the idea of Simington giving up information to me and he was striking out quickly and violently.

But he wasn't scaring me off. He was forcing me to deal with him.

Staring at the smoke and fire and destruction that Landon Keene had brought to my life and feeling the ache that had taken up permanent residence in my gut, I knew my decision was made.

SIXTY-TWO

The fire department needed most of the day to clean up the alley. Carter waved me off when I offered him a ride home, mumbling something about the walk being good for his head. I felt guilty about the car, but relieved he hadn't been in it. I'd already lost Liz. I didn't want to lose my best friend, too.

I went to bed, thinking I'd make a run at Moffitt in the morning. I still wasn't sure how that was going to work, but he was where I needed to start. And to start was better than to keep thinking.

But when I opened my door to leave the next morning, the media had discovered me.

A well-groomed Hispanic man was standing in my way, his fist raised, about to knock.

"Mr. Braddock?" he asked with a smile. "Cesar Grotillo, Channel Eight News. Do you have a moment?"

The knot in my stomach tightened like someone was yanking on one end of it. "No."

"Russell Simington is your father. Is that correct?"

Now the knot seemed tied to a freight train.

"Are you aware that he is to be executed in two days?" he asked.

I said nothing.

"Mr. Braddock? Would you care to comment?"

I slammed the door.

It happened four more times in the next two hours. I should have expected the attention. California had rarely followed through with executions since the state had reinstituted the death penalty in the early eighties. Any death at San Quentin was big news, and the media was diligent in finding anyone attached in any way.

I was attached.

And, now, with the media trying to capture every move I made, going after Keene had become even more difficult.

Carter showed up around noon. He walked in with a scowl on his face.

"What the fuck is going on out there?" he said, throwing a thumb over his shoulder to the alley.

"They know," I said. "About Simington."

"Oh," he said. "Want me to run them off?"

"Nah. It's fine. They've stopped knocking on the door."

"Simington's all over the TV, too," he said.

"I figured. That's why I haven't turned it on." I picked up an envelope off the kitchen counter and handed it to him. "For you."

"For me? For what?"

"Your car."

"Noah, man, no. You don't have to—"

Insurance wouldn't cover the car and my guilt. "Yes, I do. It's yours. I'm sorry it happened."

He didn't open the envelope, just shoved it in the back pocket of his shorts. "Alright. Thanks."

I nodded. "I want to go see Moffitt, but I don't see how we get out of here without them following."

"No way we can bail right now," he said. "They're all up and down the alley. Think they'll stay the night?"

"Some maybe, but not all of them," I said. "Probably go home and come back first thing in the morning."

"So we could get out tonight and be up there in the morning."

"Yeah."

"And I had an idea," he said.

"An idea?"

"About how to handle Moffitt. To make sure you get what you need from him."

"Let's hear it."

He told me his plan. I liked it. And I hadn't thought of anything else.

"Let's do it," I said.

He went to the door. "Okay. I'll get what we need. Why don't you call me around midnight and tell me what it looks like around here. I can pick you up a couple of blocks away or something. I'll have a ride by then."

"Alright." I hesitated. "Hey. You don't have to do this. I can do it alone. I don't know how it's gonna go and I don't want—"

He held up a big hand. "Stop right there. Liz and I . . . we weren't close. But you and she were. That's enough for me." He nodded like he'd said all that mattered. "Call me around midnight."

SIXTY-THREE

It took two more nights before I could shake free. The police had no luck in finding Keene, even after I shared my belief that he was responsible for the destruction of Carter's car. He was running free somewhere.

The media had made themselves at home on the boardwalk and in the alley. I tried to get out once to go to the grocery store, but I was immediately swarmed and I retreated inside. The vans were spending the night in the alley—anytime I stepped outside, even in the middle of the night, someone on watch snapped to life.

I was fed up with being trapped in my own house and told Carter I was getting out that night, regardless of who followed me. We made plans to meet five blocks away a little after midnight. The boardwalk was empty, and I walked all the way down to the shoreline and then up the beach before turning back up and getting out onto Mission. My long way around worked, and I arrived out on the street alone.

Carter pulled up in a Ford F-250 pickup, the huge diesel engine idling like a plane's as I opened the door.

"Yours?" I asked as I stepped up and into the cab.

"Sort of," he said, shrugging.

I reminded myself not to ask.

We made the drive out to Bareva in under an hour, thanks to the time of night. The casino was lit up like Christmas, and the parking lot was nearly full.

Cha-ching.

We parked at the far end of the lot, and Carter shut off the engine.

"We just nap now?" Carter asked.

I nodded. "Yeah. Nothing to do until morning." I glanced at him. "You got what you need?"

He pointed his thumb toward the rear window and the bed of the truck. "Back there."

I twisted around and saw a black tarp with a few shapes barely visible beneath it.

"Wake me when you're ready," he said, slouching down and closing his eyes.

SIXTY-FOUR

I figured hanging out in the casino would be a good way to get Benjamin Moffitt's attention.

I woke Carter at nine and told him I was going in. He shook the sleep out of his eyes and said he'd do his thing. I walked away from the truck, wondering if we could pull it off.

I roamed the gaming floor for an hour, keeping an eye out for anyone and anything that looked familiar. Walking in slow circles, I watched as the hardcore gamblers mixed with the day tourists who made the drive out to Bareva. I couldn't help but wonder if Simington ever gambled at any of these machines.

After walking around for a little while longer, I took the elevators up to the fourth floor, where Carter and I had gone the first time. The same receptionist greeted me.

"Good morning, sir."

"Ben Moffitt."

"I'm sorry sir, but—"

"You told me the same thing a couple of weeks ago," I said, my voice sounding hollow. "Get on the phone and tell him Braddock isn't leaving until I talk to him."

She hesitated.

"Now!" I yelled at her.

She jumped in her seat but picked up the phone. Thirty seconds later, the elevators opened behind me and Gus and Ross emerged.

Gus was still sporting a bandage along his left temple.

"Let's go," Ross said.

"You take me anywhere but to Moffitt and I'll make hitting him with a pitcher look like fun," I said, walking toward the elevator.

They stepped into the elevator behind me, and the doors closed. Ross pushed an unnumbered button, and the car began to rise.

Gus crowded in closer to me. "You think you're a badass 'cause you got off one shot? Why don't you—"

I pivoted and drove my fist into his midsection. He gasped, and I brought the heel of my hand up under his jaw. His teeth clacked shut, and blood spurted out his mouth, probably from biting his tongue. I hit him again in the stomach, and he slumped to the floor.

I swiveled toward Ross. "You wanna go?"

Ross held his hands up in surrender. "Hey, man, I'm just taking you to Mr. Moffitt's office."

I turned back to the crumpled Gus, now breathing heavily. "If you fuckin' move before I get out of this elevator, you will never move again."

Gus just continued to squeeze his eyes shut as the blood leaked out of his mouth.

I wasn't kidding. Gus had stepped into the wrong place at the wrong time. Anger was rippling through my body, and I didn't need an excuse to unleash it.

The elevator came to a halt, and the doors opened. I stepped out. The doors closed and sent Gus away.

Ross and I walked down the corridor toward Moffitt's office and found him sitting behind his desk.

He looked up and smiled. "Mr. Braddock, nice to see you again." He glanced past me at Ross. "Thank you, Ross. That will be all."

Ross looked concerned, like maybe he should mention that I'd flattened Gus in the elevator. But he wasn't confident enough to stand up to his boss's dismissal. He hesitated, then sort of shrugged and left, closing the office doors behind him.

"So, Mr. Braddock," Moffitt said. "What can I do for you today?"

"You're going to tell me about Landon Keene," I said.

A moment of forced confusion flickered through his features. "I think you mentioned his name last time and—"

I walked around the desk, grabbed him by the shirt, and lifted him out of the leather chair. Shock registered on his face, and he slapped at my hands. I shoved him over to the window and banged his forehead on the glass.

"Look carefully," I said.

"What?" Moffitt said, his voice frantic. "What?"

"Two hundred yards in front of you," I said. "Do you see him?"

He steadied himself, now looking out the window, probably wondering what the hell he was supposed to see. Then he said, "Jesus Christ."

"That's right," I said, glancing up and spotting Carter outside, aiming the rifle right at us. "I'm going to let you go, but you aren't going to move. If you do, he's going to make your head a convertible before you get more than a foot. Do you understand?"

"Jesus Christ," he repeated.

"I seriously doubt he will be the one to greet you in the afterlife. Do you understand me?"

"Yes! Shit, yes! I get it."

"And if anyone barges in here and you don't tell them to get the fuck out, I'm going to signal to him and he's going to kill you. Do you understand that?"

Sweat was running down his cheeks. "Yeah, I understand."

"Don't pull your forehead off that glass," I said. "Don't move until I tell you to."

"Alright! What the fuck do you want from me?"

"Tell me about Landon Keene."

His eyes were dancing back and forth between me and the rifle pointed at him from two hundred yards away. "What do you want to know?"

"He works for you?"

"No. Yes. He's blackmailing me."

That surprised me. "How?"

He was bent over at an awkward angle, but he was as still as a statue. "I pay him. He works out of my casino."

"Works out of your casino. Hiring coyotes?"

His eyes shifted in my direction. "Yes."

"Are you involved in his smuggling operation?"

"I was. I got out a few years ago as I was getting into the casinos. That's what he's holding over me," he said. "It overlapped for a while.

He says he'll go to the gaming board and let them know about my past if I don't let him do his thing."

That made sense. Moffitt didn't need the smuggling money because the casino money was worlds better. But one wrong turn and it could all disappear.

"My back is killing me," he said. "Can I stand up?"

"Do it slowly, but don't turn away from the glass. Keep your eyes on our friend out there."

Moffitt moved like he was in slow motion, rising until he was in an upright position. He kept his forehead on the glass.

"What about Russell Simington?" I asked.

He took a deep breath, looking for any measure of composure. "The three of us worked together. Keene, Simington, and myself. Smuggling. Keene and I worked together at first. He wanted to put together a larger operation. I wanted out, to do other things. I got interested in the casinos, he stayed with the smuggling. Keene was always the brains, the driving force."

"You employed Simington, too?"

"Yes. But only because Keene made me. He wanted him working in the casinos to help scout."

I believed him because it all fit together.

"When did you get out?" I asked.

"After Simington got arrested," he said. "I'd made enough, and it was getting too dangerous. I got in on the gaming contracts with the money I'd made from running the Mexicans and was able to open two more casinos. I didn't need it anymore." He let out a sigh. "Keene came to me a year later and wanted to use the casinos. More casinos meant more recruiting for him, more potential targets. I said no, and he threatened to ruin me. I gave in."

All of what he was saying put things in line for me. But at that moment, I didn't care about getting things in line. I only wanted one thing.

"Where do I find Keene?" I asked.

"Oh, man," he said, getting close to a whine. "Come on."

"One signal from me and he puts one bullet in your face," I reminded Moffitt.

The perspiration cascaded down his red cheeks. "Shit. Alright. I don't know where he lives. He jumps from house to house. But I know he's going to El Centro tomorrow."

El Centro. A little spark went off in my head. "Why?"

"I'm not sure. He said he was going down there for a few days. That he had to go tie up some loose ends."

Loose ends. The widow of a man he had murdered.

"Why has what happened there become so important to him?" I said, as much to myself as to Moffitt. "Why is he now so determined to close the whole thing up?"

"I don't know," Moffitt said, glancing at me.

I nodded at the window. "I think his finger is getting twitchy on the trigger. Try again. Why now?"

Moffitt swallowed hard. "He said something about a woman talking to a cop."

Lucia. And Asanti. And Keene was probably worried that she was telling him about the extortion attempt and that she might be able to tie him to Simington. I wasn't clear on what was setting Keene off, but it seemed to me that while he was confident that he had Moffitt and Simington leveraged, he feared anything I might learn.

Loose ends.

I stepped in close to Moffitt. I held two fingers up to the window, and I saw Carter nod in the distance.

"I just told him I'll be outside in two minutes," I said. "If you move before he lowers that gun, he will shoot you. If I'm not out in two minutes, he will shoot you." I leaned in close. "And if you talk to Keene before I find him, if I find out you told anyone about our conversation, I will get to you and make you wish he had shot you. Got it?"

He nodded, his forehead squeaking against the window. "Yes."

I hoped I never had to set eyes on Benjamin Moffitt again.

SIXTY-FIVE

Carter had the truck waiting in front of the casino when I walked out the front like I'd just finished testing my luck. Which I guess I had.

"He didn't move, so I suppose it went okay?" he said as we drove off.

"Keene is going to be in El Centro. Tomorrow."

"Why?"

"Vasquez's wife?" I said. "Moffitt said something about him tying up loose ends. He must know she's still there."

"He could be going down just to do business. Maybe he's bringing over another load."

Carter could have been right, but I doubted it. The timing was too coincidental. The week of Simington's execution, Keene was heading back to where it all began. He was probably assuming that everyone would be so wrapped up in Simington's impending death that he could slip down south, do what he needed to do, and slip out unnoticed. Make sure that everything went to the grave with Simington.

I'm sure he thought it was a good plan.

And if I hadn't learned about it, it would have been even better.

WEEK FOUR

SIXTY-SIX

Carter and I spent the rest of the day making plans. We needed some things to take with us, and we needed a second car. I rented a Chevy Impala rather than risk going back to my place to get my Jeep.

By the time we pulled off the freeway into El Centro, midnight was descending on the Imperial Valley. The moonlight threw shadows over the gravel and sand as we drove down the road toward the Vasquez house. I shut the visions of Liz out of my head as I parked the rental in front of the home.

I didn't want to ring the doorbell in the middle of the night, and I figured no one would attempt entering with two strange cars parked in front of the house. Carter and I tried to sleep in the cab of his truck but ended up taking turns dozing more than anything else.

At eight the next morning, Carter and I went up the front walk and I rapped on the screen door. The front door opened and Lucia Vasquez looked at us, her expression puzzled for a moment before recognition filtered onto her face. "Mr. Braddock?"

"I'm sorry to disturb you, Mrs. Vasquez," I said, then gestured at Carter. "This is my friend Carter Hamm."

They exchanged nods.

"May we come in for a moment?" I asked.

She looked reluctant.

"Please," I said. "It's important."

She pressed her lips together, then held the screen door open for us. We stepped in past her.

The television was on in the living room, the volume turned down.

"My boys," she said. "They are still asleep." She pointed at the sofa. "Please, sit down."

We sat, and she moved into the chair across from us, sitting on the edge. "Why are you here?"

"The man who arranged to bring Hernando here," I said. "Landon Keene. Have you heard from him?"

Her features immediately filled with alarm. "No. No. Why?"

"I think he's looking for you," I said. "I believe he's on his way here."

She brought her hands to her chest. "What? Why?"

"I'm not sure," I said. "But I feel certain he's coming here. To your home."

She whispered something in Spanish, then looked at me. "I won't let him hurt my boys. I won't."

I nodded. "I won't either. That's why I'm here. I'd like for you and the boys to go with Carter. I hope just for today, but it might be longer. He'll make sure you are safe."

She looked at Carter, who remained expressionless.

"I'll stay here and see what happens," I said. "When I know it's safe to come back, I'll let you know."

"Should we call the police?" she asked. "Detective Asanti?"

"I think it's better if we keep them out of this at the moment," I said. "I don't want to bring any unnecessary attention to your family."

I was using her situation to get myself in the situation I wanted to be in. It wasn't fair, and what I'd said wasn't necessarily true. But it had the desired effect.

She stood. "I will go wake the boys." She left the room.

Carter watched her go down the hall. "You'll be alright here?" he asked. "If he shows up, you'll be alright?"

I waited for Lucia Vasquez and her boys to return, not knowing how to answer that question.

SIXTY-SEVEN

For three days, I wandered around the Vasquez home, looking at pictures, checking closets, waiting. Periodically I called Carter, making sure all was okay. They were twenty minutes away, in a hotel in Yuma, safe. The kids thought they were on vacation. Lucia seemed concerned but was making the best of it.

On the fourth day, I was beginning to think that what Carter had suggested was true. Maybe Keene was just coming down to attend to other business and I'd overreacted. Maybe he'd assumed that Liz's death had sent me into a downward spiral since I'd disappeared and he was in the clear. Maybe I had unnecessarily disrupted the Vasquezes' lives for my own agenda. But I'd told him about my conversation with Klimes and he'd gone through the trouble to blow up Carter's car. I just didn't think he'd run. It didn't fit with everything else he'd done.

I decided to sit through one more night. Then, if nothing had happened, I'd call it off.

The house was mortuary quiet for most of the evening, just like all the previous nights. A few creaks and hums in the dark, but nothing more. I sat in the far corner of the living room, listening to the tiny sounds, wondering if Keene was coming.

It was just past four in the morning when I stopped wondering.

At first, I wasn't sure I'd heard anything. I listened hard and it was quiet. But then I made out the faint scrape of a footstep outside the front door.

I lay down next to the couch, pressing myself into the floor. My eyes had adjusted enough to the dim light that I could see the doorknob move. It jiggled, the hand on the other side slowly working it back and forth. Finally, it gave.

I steadied the 9mm in my hands and aimed right at the door.

The door inched open, and initially it seemed no one was there. But my eyes focused, and I could see Keene dressed entirely in black. He'd made the mistake of coming in without his gun drawn. He shut the door behind him, not a sound coming from him or the door.

He turned away from the door and eyed the hallway. If Lucia and the boys had been there, Keene would've smiled and thought about how clever he was.

I squeezed the trigger and the quiet of the house exploded. The bullet hit Keene's thigh with a wet thud, and he collapsed.

I vaulted off the floor and was on top of him immediately. His hands were grasping at his leg, and his eyes were wide with shock. I dropped my knee onto his thigh where I thought the wound was, and he howled. I slapped a hand across his mouth.

"Hurts, doesn't it?" I said, grinding my knee harder into his leg.

He strained against me, ugly groans echoing against the palm of my hand.

"See you in a little bit," I said, then dropped the butt of my gun into his temple.

SIXTY-EIGHT

I drove east on the highway, then south without a road, until we were out in the middle of the dark desert. Keene was still unconscious in the passenger seat. I opened the door and threw him to the ground.

He rolled over with a grunt, his left thigh decorated with a wide swath of dark blood. I pulled out the garbage bags I'd lined the interior of the rental car with and tossed them in a pile next to him.

His eyes opened slowly.

I fired the Sig Sauer Carter had obtained for me about a foot from Keene's left ear. He jerked and rolled hard to his right. He came face up again, dirt and sand now caked in the bleeding gash above his eye.

"You killed Darcy," I said and fired again at the ground, this time to his right. My voice sounded unusually loud in the silent and lonely desert.

He yelled and rolled in the opposite direction. He pushed up on his hands and sat up, his breathing ragged.

"You left my father to rot in prison," I said.

Keene tensed, waiting for another shot. I surprised him with a roundhouse kick to the jaw and felt the bone snap as I drove my foot through the kick. He fell to the side, his hands coming to his face.

I dropped to my knees and pulled him up. He grunted, and a weird smile came over his busted-up face. Even knowing he was near the end of his life, Keene was arrogant.

I held onto his shirt, our faces two feet apart. "And you killed the only person who has ever really mattered to me."

The tears welled up in my eyes. I looked away for a moment, angry that I was showing him how much he had hurt me and that I couldn't get a handle on my emotions. I waited, willing my control to return.

I took a deep breath and looked at him through my blurred, salty vision.

I don't know what he was thinking. Maybe that I would drag it out, make him tell me more things that I wanted to know. But we were beyond that.

I tugged on his shirt and brought our faces together, shoving the gun against the middle of his sternum. He was gasping but too weak to pull away. He coughed, and the sound echoed across the desert floor.

And yet the uncomfortable smile remained on his face, letting me know that no matter what was about to happen, he had still won part of the battle.

For a second, I thought about ending it. Leaving it all and walking away. Be the stronger person. Do the right thing, like Liz had said.

But I no longer had a grasp on the difference between right and wrong. It all melted into one big mountain of hurt and pain and emptiness.

The smile on his face grew a fraction.

I squeezed the trigger and emptied the gun into Landon Keene's chest.

SIXTY-NINE

"I don't see it," Carter said.

"Me either."

We were standing in the middle of the desert. I'd called him and told him they could come back. He'd taken the Vasquezes to their home and then found me.

I'd buried Keene, and we were looking for any visible signs that there was a grave in the middle of nowhere.

"Then we're good," Carter said.

That was about as far from the truth as we could get.

"We should go separately," Carter said. "Call me when you get there."

I nodded.

He walked to the truck and slid in through the passenger side. The engine started with a low rumble. He nodded at me, drove up onto the road, and disappeared.

I turned to the valley and stared hard.

The sun was coming up.

Just like before.

I stared again. It was a remote location, not a place people went hiking or off-roading. But people would start looking for Keene.

Even assholes have friends.

The sand and isolation would hide him for a while.

I just wondered for how long.

SEVENTY

I drove back to San Diego feeling numb and empty. All of things that I had vaguely hoped I might feel once Keene was gone were non-existent. And I kept thinking of Liz, somewhere, watching me and shaking her head, telling me I'd screwed up.

I knew I needed to bring the whole thing full circle, to find some sort of closure, no matter how forced or pointless.

I went straight to the airport and bought a ticket to San Francisco. Simington had about twelve hours left in his life, and I thought I needed to be there for one of them.

The fact that the sun was shining in San Francisco when I landed completed the whole reverse axis the planet seemed to be spinning on. No clouds, no fog, no haze. Just sunshine lying across the water in some sort of alternate universe.

I called San Quentin and managed to arrange a visit for mid-afternoon. I rented a car and, with some time to waste, drove to a place I'd always wanted to see.

Forty-five minutes later I was perched on a cliff watching waves the size of buildings rise out of the ocean. A group of six was out in the frigid water, along with two more guys on jet-skis toting huge cameras.

Maverick's was arguably one of the most dangerous surf spots on the planet. It had gone undiscovered for a long time until a guy named Jeff Clark paddled out and realized he'd found a gold mine, albeit one laced with dynamite. The waves rose out of the harbor in monstrous heights and then broke onto a wall of rocks that were sharpened like razors and axes. If you managed to survive a fall onto the rocks, you were just as likely to get your board tangled in the jagged reef beneath the surface of the water. All the while, the massive waves kept breaking on your head like hammers.

Brutal.

But the waves looked like they were drawn by an artist, with faces like ski slopes.

Hard to resist.

I didn't have any plans to get in the water. I didn't have the right equipment nor did I have the right mindset. You had to be totally dialed in to paddle out, and as pretty as the waves looked, I knew that my head was too much of a mess even to give it a shot. But sitting on the cliff, watching those who knew what they were doing, felt like a brief escape from the rest of my world.

There were maybe twenty of us watching. The rare sunny winter afternoon had brought out folks who knew there'd be a show. Any other time in my life, I would have called Carter on my cell and told him what I was watching. He'd been talking about Maverick's for years. Knowing that I was sitting above the water would have killed him, and I would have enjoyed hearing him whine.

But even that didn't sound fun.

Two boys, maybe sixteen, came up and sat down on the rocks next to me. Shorts and T-shirts with surf company logos. Uncombed hair and year-round tans. Probably what I had looked like at their age. They were pointing and grinning. Their excitement was tangible.

The nearest one glanced at me. "Any idea who's out there?"

I shook my head. "Nah. Just got here."

"We heard Mel was gonna be out," the other one said, scanning the lineup.

Peter Mel was a local and one of the greatest big-wave surfers of his era. He had helped get Maverick's onto the map. Among other surfers, he was a rock star.

"Really?" I said, looking to the water. "Didn't know that."

"We saw him out here two weeks ago," the nearest one said, his face busting into an electric grin. "Man, he was just awesome."

I smiled, and it felt awkward. "I'll bet."

"I don't see him," the other one said.

"Bummer," his pal said, but he didn't really seem that disappointed.

The waves smashed to the surface with a ferociousness I had never seen. It sounded like a train wreck every time one of them closed out, a mixture of chaos and beauty. We watched a surfer paddle into one that looked twenty-five feet high. The wave picked him up and launched him down the face. Against the huge wall of water, he looked like a flea on a dog's back. He raced along the bottom of the wave, the water crashing behind him on the fall line. Right before the wave closed out over him, he shot up its face and jettisoned over the lip, saving himself the torture of being caught beneath the falling behemoth.

Several of the spectators on the cliff clapped. The boys high-fived.

A cell phone rang, and the kid nearest me reached for his pocket and extracted the ringing phone. "Hey."

He listened for a few seconds, kind of rolled his eyes. "Yeah. No. Me and Denny are out at Maverick's."

Denny laughed on the other side of him.

"I know," the kid was saying. "Yeah, but . . . I will. I swear."

Then he held the phone out as far away as possible and made a face at it.

He pulled it back to his ear. "I'll call you as soon as we leave, okay?"

He punched the phone off and slid it back into his pocket and glanced at me. "My girlfriend."

"Ah."

"She doesn't surf," he said with a sigh. "She doesn't get it. Thinks we're just wasting time out here."

I thought about my own experiences. Liz hadn't always surfed. It was just beginning to become something we shared. But she'd never acted like she didn't understand.

A sudden pang of loneliness struck my gut. She and I weren't ever going to be in the water together again.

"Sometimes it takes awhile," I said.

"I'm not sure," the kid said, a skeptical look on his face.

I watched one last wave pulverize the rider, crushing him beneath a falling wall of white water.

I stood and put my hand on the kid's shoulder.

"Give her time," I said. "Or she'll be gone before you know it."

SEVENTY-ONE

The prison looked different.

When I'd visited last, it had looked sullen and isolated. Now, it resembled a shopping mall on the weekend.

Gathered near the main entrance were maybe five hundred people holding signs and candles. They seemed to be equally divided between those calling for Simington's death and those who were opposed. The scene was calm at the moment, but I knew as the day wore on, the tension would grow.

I spotted Kenney lurking at the perimeter of the crowd. He saw me, too, nodded in greeting, and walked toward me.

"Surprised to see you," he said.

"Yeah," I said. "Not really sure why I'm here."

"They letting you in to see him?"

"I called earlier and set it up."

Kenney shoved his hands in his pockets and lifted his chin in the direction of the cameras and crowd. "These clowns know who you are?"

"They did in San Diego. Hoping they don't up here."

"If they swarm you, I'll come run interference," he said.

"Thanks."

We stood there, awkwardness filling the space between us.

"I'm not sorry for him," he said. "But I'm sorry you have to go in there."

I understood what he was getting at, and I appreciated the effort. But at the same time, if he'd known what I'd done earlier in the day, I didn't think we'd be having the same kind of conversation.

"Thanks," I told him. "I'm gonna head in."

He held out his hand. "Good luck."

We shook, and I nodded without saying anything. Kenney turned and walked back to where I'd first spotted him. He put his arm around a woman whom I'd failed to see initially. She leaned into him, her head on his shoulder.

His sister.

One more victim.

I looked at the prison and went in for the final time.

SEVENTY-TWO

Security was tighter. I was patted down twice, and my ID was checked three times. I was led to a different area this time, a room off the hallway past the usual visitors' area. The room was about twenty by twenty, with a table in the middle and several folding chairs.

Simington sat in one of the chairs, a plate with a huge hamburger and a pile of French fries in front of him. Two guards, at opposite ends of the room, watched him with the same pleasure they might watch a late-night infomercial.

He smiled and gestured at the plate. "All day. I get pretty much whatever I want. I've got a pizza, a lasagna, a plate of pancakes, and a six pack of Pepsi coming in tonight for the last one."

When I'd called to arrange the visit, they'd told me he'd be in a different room, but I wasn't prepared to be so close to him. Not having the glass between us was unnerving. The barrier had provided a buffer for me, something that kept me from realizing he was a real person. Without it, I couldn't escape that he was a living, breathing human being.

About to die.

I slid into the metal folding chair across the table from him. "That's great."

He stuffed a fry into his mouth and nodded. "Like they're trying to make up for what they're about to do to me. Oh well, huh?"

There was no anxiety or nervousness about him. His repeated statements that he was fine with all this seemed proven by his attitude and his appetite.

"I guess," I said.

He wiped his mouth with a napkin. "Surprised you came back. Thought we were done the last time."

"Me, too."

He folded his arms across his chest, the tattoo on his wrist flashing at me like a neon sign. "So. You take care of things in San Diego?"

I hesitated, then nodded. "Yeah."

"Good for you," he said, his voice lower now.

"Not really."

"Yes, it is. It needed to get done."

Discussing a murder in a prison was doing nothing to alleviate the tension in my body and my mind.

"Been a long time coming," Simington said. "Never thought it would happen, really." A thin, dry smile appeared on his face. "Almost didn't, I guess. But I knew I could count on you." He reached for one of the hamburgers.

Knew I could count on you.

It had been sticking in my skin for the previous two weeks. Why had he sent Darcy to me in the first place when he'd had no intention of fighting his sentence? Why had he talked to me when he'd spoken to no one else? Why had he thrown out Keene's name in the first place? His answers had always seemed hollow, but I'd accepted them at the time. Maybe because I'd been looking for some sort of connection with him. Maybe because I'd wanted to believe that some part of him was good. But somewhere in my head and in my heart, I knew there was something else, something much less altruistic, in his actions. And now, finally, I heard it in his words.

"This is what you wanted from the first day, isn't it?" I asked.

The hamburger was halfway to his mouth. "What?"

"You didn't give a shit about me," I said, seeing it all again in my head. "You wanted Keene."

He set the burger back on the plate and wiped his hands on the thighs of his pants. "What are you talking about?"

"You were never going to work with Darcy," I said. "You sent her to me to get to Keene. And then you sent me after him."

He leaned back in the chair and said nothing.

"Gave me just enough to keep me going," I said, shaking my head at how stupid I'd been. "Just pointing me in the right direction."

Simington cleared his throat and fixed his eyes on me. "Some things need to get done."

His voice had dropped an octave, like someone had poured sawdust down his throat. His eyes had hollowed out. And I finally saw the man whom everyone had talked about. The thug, the killer, the man who belonged on death row.

"You used me," I said.

"You let me use you."

"Fuck you."

He laughed. "Whatever it takes. That son of a bitch was gonna die before I did. I just seized an opportunity."

I thought of Darcy and Liz. They had died because Simington had been looking for revenge. Revenge that I had carried out for him.

"You'll find another girlfriend, Noah," he said. "That's what you're really upset about. It'll pass."

It was like his words were on tape and they'd gotten stuck in the player, coming out slow and garbled. I ran them through my head again to make sure I'd heard him correctly.

"How do you know about her?" I asked, an invisible spear digging into my spine.

"What?" he said. Something flashed across his face. He realized he'd made a mistake.

I was rewinding the tape in my head. The last time I'd been there, Kenney had said something that hadn't made sense to me. Something about Simington having old friends visit him. Visitors.

"Keene came to see you," I said, as much for me to hear as for Simington.

"Noah, look—"

"What did he tell you about her?" I asked, the spear digging in further.

He hesitated for a moment, probably trying to decide whether he should keep up the act. I could almost see the mental shrug, him deciding it wasn't worth the effort. His face hardened. "He told me you were dating a cop."

"Did he threaten her?"

"Does it matter?"

The anger was building, but I tried to remain calm. "Did Keene threaten her?"

He watched me, then nodded.

"And you didn't tell me? When I was here last time, you didn't tell me?"

He folded his arms across his chest. "Keene came here to scare me. Fuckin' moron." He waved his hand around the room. "Thinking I'd be scared of him after living here. He was pissing his pants if he was crazy enough to walk in here and be seen with me."

I sat there, staring at him, my legs starting to shake.

"That son of a bitch told me if you didn't back off, he was gonna take her out," he said, his eyes empty. "He thought that would do something for me, make me rethink talking to you. I think he feared me just enough to not go directly after you. But he thought threatening your girlfriend might shake things up."

The shivers moved from my legs up my spine.

"Well, it did, but not the way he thought," he said, chuckling.

"You didn't tell me," I whispered.

"Hell, no, I didn't tell you," he said. "I wanted Keene to go after her. I needed something to kick you in the ass. I could see you didn't have it in you. I thought that might be it." His smile contained a million little daggers. "And I was right."

I jumped out of the chair at him, but he was ready. In one smooth motion, his arm swept around my neck and he brought my head down onto his knee like he was slamming a door shut. Colors exploded behind my eyes, and pain rocketed through my head and neck.

I fell to the floor. Voices and heavy footsteps echoed around me. I rolled over onto my back. Simington was bent over the table, a guard on either side of him, his hands already in cuffs. One of the guards was talking into the mic wired into his shirt.

Blood leaked into my right eye. The impact had opened a gash above my eyebrow, and I could feel the air sucking into the gap in my skin.

Another guard helped me up. "Are you alright, sir?"

"I'm fine," I said, dizzy and disoriented.

"You're going to need to go to the infirmary," he said.

Simington was smiling at me as the two guards raised him off the table.

"I'm fine," I repeated.

"We'll see what they say at the infirmary, sir," the guard said, slipping his hand behind my arm and steadying me.

"Sorry, son," Simington said. "Sorry that it had to end like this."

The blood stung my eye but I didn't lift a hand to wipe it away. Carolina had warned me.

Don't let him hurt you now.

I'd failed there, too. He'd hurt me in several unimaginable ways, ways that were going to leave lifetime scars.

Simington chuckled again as the guards escorted him out of the room, my last vision of him blurred and bloody.

SEVENTY-THREE

The nurse in the prison infirmary wanted to stitch the cut, but I refused, not wanting to spend any more time there than I had to. She closed it with a butterfly bandage and urged me to reconsider getting the stitches.

I left without saying a word.

My flight back to San Diego was delayed. I sat in the airport fingering the bandage and trying not to watch the news coverage on the overhead television monitors, most of it focusing on Simington's impending execution, now hours away. The crowd outside the prison had multiplied since I'd left.

Two hours behind schedule, the airline personnel finally boarded us. I slid into my window seat.

It was dark now outside, the tiny runway lights blinking as we taxied. The plane paused as we positioned for takeoff.

San Francisco had not been kind to me. It wasn't the city's fault, but I would always associate it with the ugliest time in my life.

My breathing sped up. I tried to slow it, but I couldn't.

The plane accelerated, pressing me back into my seat.

My fingers went to the bandage, feeling the gauze and tape and what Simington had done to me. And to Darcy and to Liz.

We lifted off the ground and I felt it all—all of the things that I'd gone through the last few weeks—catch me like a sucker punch from an invisible fist. I squeezed my eyes shut, trying to push it away.

The plane angled upward and turned.

I opened my eyes and looked out the window, the tears obscuring everything I was saying goodbye to.

SEVENTY-FOUR

My cell phone rang as soon as I turned it on, stepping off the Jetway in San Diego. I recognized Carter's number and answered. "Hey."

"Where are you?" he asked, his voice urgent.

"Just got back. Walking to my car."

"From where?"

"San Francisco."

"They found him."

I moved over to the wall, out of the flow of foot traffic. "How do you know?"

"It was on the news an hour ago," he said. "Hikers coming back from camping in the desert. They found him. Tried to call you, but I guess you were on the plane."

I took a deep breath. "Okay."

"I'm gonna lay low for a few days, see what shakes out," he said. "We should be fine, but I don't wanna take any chances."

"That's fine."

"I'll call you," he said and hung up.

I dropped the phone into my pocket. I didn't know what I expected to feel, but Carter's call hadn't surprised me. I wasn't entirely sure the police could tie Keene to us, but I knew where they'd coming looking first. It wasn't a comfortable feeling.

I drove home in the rain, thinking about that, wondering what I should do.

The ideas were ticking through my head when I walked into my living room and found John Wellton sitting on the couch, in the dark.

"Where you been?" he asked.

I thought about asking him how he'd gotten in, but I didn't see the point. "San Francisco."

"What happened to your eye?"

"Nothing."

I stood there in the dark, looking at him.

"We found Keene," he said.

"Really?"

"Yeah. Dead. Outside of El Centro."

"Shame."

He stood and walked over to the glass slider, the rain slithering down the door. "One of El Centro's guys was there. Named Asanti."

My stomach lurched. "Oh."

"Says you guys know each other."

"Yeah."

"Klimes and Zanella are working the scene with him," he said. "They interviewed a woman named Lucia Vasquez."

A huge flash of lightening exploded over the ocean and lit the whole room for a moment.

My throat went dry, and my fingers felt cold and heavy.

"Asanti says you know her, too."

I kept my mouth shut.

"She says you came to her home a few nights ago. That a friend of yours—a big guy—took her and her boys to a motel. So she'd be safe." He paused. "She says you told her Keene was coming to her home."

My heart pounded like it wanted out of my chest, like I was keeping it captive.

He turned to me. "I'll give you two hours."

"What?"

"They sent me to find you, Noah," he said, his voice thick. "I'll give you two hours before I start looking. Gives you a head start to get out of here."

"Look, Wellton—"

He raised a hand. "Don't, alright? Just don't. I understand why you did it. I asked you to call me, but you didn't. The less you say the better." He took a deep breath and exhaled. "I'll see what I can do, but for now, you need to get out of here and disappear. Unless you want to go down. Klimes is already champing at the bit to talk to you."

I felt like vomiting. It was all slipping away from me, and there was no way for me to hold on to it.

But, then, what was really left for me to hold onto?

Wellton walked past me to the front door and opened it. "I can only put them off for so long. Don't be a fool. Get out of here. And I don't mean hole up with your pal. I mean get fucking lost." He stepped out into the rain.

I sat down on the couch and watched the clock over the television tick away. I could stay and deny it all. There was no guarantee they'd have enough to tie me to Keene's death. But what Lucia Vasquez knew was pretty damning. Klimes and Zanella had motive, and they knew I'd been there.

I didn't want to go to jail. Didn't want to be like Simington. Like my father. But maybe it was too late for that. It seemed that the more I had tried to distance myself from him, the more I had become like him.

You're not him, Liz had said.

Maybe I wasn't when she said it, but I sure seemed to fit the bill now.

The hands on the clock lay across each other and pointed at the twelve. Midnight.

Simington would be strapped in now. The syringe would be readied. Maybe two more minutes in his life.

How many were left in mine?

The Last Day of February

I wondered how it had come to this.
No. That wasn't right.
I knew exactly how it had come to this.

Lightning shattered the sky and raked the black surface of the ocean. The rain spilling out from above hit my face and body like a shower as I stood on my patio, soaking me and the duffel bag slung over my shoulder. The water stung the cut above my eye and grew the bloody stain on my shirt.

I knew that I wouldn't ever stand on this patio again, stare at this view again, live in this home again.

Thunder rolled off the Pacific like it was coming through a megaphone, rattling the windows and doors of all the homes on the boardwalk. The rain picked up velocity, splashing violently into the puddles on the ground.

I wiped the water from my eyes and took another look, making sure that all of it—my home, the view, this world I had created for myself—would never leave my memory.

I knew that it wouldn't, just as I knew that the last month would never leave me either.

Things like that don't leave you. They inhabit you. Forever.

I turned to the glass door and squinted through the reflected bands of rain. My gun lay on the kitchen table. Two surfboards stood in the corner. Most everything I owned was still inside. I didn't know what would happen to those things. And I didn't care.

The lightning cracked again behind me. A starter's pistol, telling me it was time to go.

I stepped off the patio and headed for the car, leaving the remains of my life behind.